Fort

Cynthia DeFelice

SQUARE
FISH

Farrar Straus Giroux

New York

SQUARE
FISH

An imprint of Macmillan Publishing Group, LLC
175 Fifth Avenue
New York, NY 10010
mackids.com

Square Fish and the Square Fish logo are trademarks of Macmillan and
are used by Farrar Straus Giroux under license from Macmillan.

Our books may be purchased in bulk for promotional, educational, or business
use. Please contact your local bookseller or the Macmillan Corporate
and Premium Sales Department at (800) 221-7945 ext. 5442 or by
e-mail at MacmillanSpecialMarkets@macmillan.com.

Library of Congress Cataloging-in-Publication Data
DeFelice, Cynthia C.
    Fort / Cynthia DeFelice.
        pages cm
    Summary: "A middle-grade summer adventure about two boys who build
an awesome fort and tangle with two older bullies"—Provided by publisher.
    ISBN 978-1-250-07973-2 (paperback)   ISBN 978-0-374-32429-2 (ebook)
    [1. Best friends—Fiction. 2. Friendship—Fiction. 3. Bullying—Fiction.
4. Summer—Fiction. 5. Great-aunts—Fiction. 6. Great-uncles—Fiction.]
I. Title.

PZ7.D3597For 2015
[Fic]—dc23

                                                                    2014040167

Originally published in the United States by Farrar Straus Giroux
First Square Fish Edition: 2016
Book designed by Andrew Arnold
Square Fish logo designed by Filomena Tuosto

                    10 9 8 7 6 5 4

                    AR: 4.4 / LEXILE: 700L

For the past denizens of the
K.C. House and forts everywhere

This is the 100 percent true story of the summer I—Wyatt Jones—was eleven and built a fort in the woods with my friend Augie Valerio.

It isn't the story I handed in to my teacher about how I spent my summer vacation. See, there's stuff that happened that you can't really talk about in school. Not unless you want to get in trouble.

Plus, there are things in here like dead squirrels. And squirrel guts. And some maggots.

There are weapons, too: a slingshot, a pellet gun, and a pocketknife.

I'm just warning you, in case that kind of stuff bothers you.

But anyway, I think it's a pretty good story, even though you know from reading this that I lived through it, which, believe me, I wasn't sure was going to happen.

1

"Aw, this is getting too easy," I said to Augie. "We need something that moves."

We were lying on our bellies shooting Augie's pellet gun at some tin cans we had lined up on a fallen log.

"Well, I guess we could get Herkimer," Augie said.

I sat up. This was interesting. Augie knew someone named Herkimer? And this Herkimer guy would let us shoot at him? "Who's Herkimer?" I asked.

"The stuffed owl in my great-uncle's attic," said Augie.

Augie's my best buddy here in upstate New York, which is where my dad and I have come to spend the past three summers. Augie's great, but sometimes it takes me a while to figure out what he's talking about.

"This owl is stuffed?" I said.

Augie nodded. "But it looks really real."

"And it *moves*?" I asked.

Augie laughed. "No, pea brain. It's *stuffed*."

I sighed. "Well, you brought it up when I was saying we need a target that *moves*."

It was Augie's turn to sigh in exasperation. "So, like I said, we put out Herkimer."

"And what? Wait for him to get struck by lightning and come back to life?"

"Man," said Augie. "I keep forgetting. You city kids don't know anything. See, crows hate owls. They see an owl and they go nuts. They all go after it, trying to make it fly away. It's called mobbing. So we put out Herkimer, the crows come, and we shoot *them*."

"Wow," I said. "Cool. So how do we get Herkimer?"

Augie frowned. "It's not going to be easy. My uncle loves that owl. He keeps him in a glass display case and everything. But my aunt says Herkimer's nasty and disgusting, so she makes Unk keep him in the attic."

"I thought you told me he was your great-uncle," I said.

"Huh? Oh, he is. But it's too hard to say 'great' every time. And my aunt—she's actually my great-aunt, but she doesn't like to be called that, because she thinks it makes her sound old—she says if I call my uncle great, he'll only get a big head and it's plenty big enough already. So I just call them aunt and uncle."

"Oh," I said, kind of wishing I hadn't asked. "So, anyway, how are we going to get the owl out of the attic?"

Augie scrunched up his face the way he did when he was thinking. So far, Augie's plan sounded like genius, and I waited to hear the rest.

"Okay," he said at last. "Here's the mission."

Augie liked to plan "missions." It made the stuff we did sound real official.

"Unk's probably down at Juliano's junkyard shooting the breeze with Al," he went on. "Since he retired, that's where he's been spending most of his time. So you just have to distract my aunt while I run up to the attic and snag Herkimer."

"Okay," I said. "So I create a diversion, right? Throw a stink bomb, something like that?"

"Yeah, cool!" said Augie, looking excited. "Ya got one?"

"A stink bomb?" I asked. "No. You?"

"No. Darn."

"Yeah."

We thought for a while.

"I know," said Augie. "What if we stop by real

casual, like we just want to say hi, you know? My aunt will probably ask if we want lemonade or cookies or something, and I can say I have to go to the bathroom, and while she's asking you how the winter was and how your dad is and all that stuff, I'll go upstairs, get Herkimer, hide him outside in the bushes, and come in again. We'll stay long enough to be polite, and then leave."

I nodded. "Sounds good. How will we get Herkimer back?"

Augie shrugged. "We'll figure that out later. You ready?"

"Ready."

We rode our bikes a little way up the gravel road to a house with the name *Hinkle* painted on a new mailbox that stood out front. I read it incredulously. "Wait," I said. "I know he's your Uncle Heindel. But is his last name really *Hinkle*?"

Augie nodded. "German side of the family."

"So he's *Heindel Hinkle*?" I repeated. "Seriously? His name is *Heindel Hinkle*? *Heindel Hinkle*?" The more I said it, the more it cracked me up. After a few seconds Augie was laughing, too, and soon we were both rolling on the Hinkle lawn in hysterics.

"Augie?" called a throaty voice. "Is that you?"

Augie looked up, his face red and his eyes tearing from laughter, and finally croaked, "Y-yes, Aunt Hilda."

"Heindel and Hilda Hinkle?" I sputtered, before collapsing in another burst of helpless laughter.

"Augie, are you all right? And is that Wyatt with you? Is he having some kind of a fit?"

Augie pulled himself together enough to whisper, "Can it, Wyatt. Come on, you've met Aunt Hilda before, haven't you?"

"Yes," I gasped. "But I never knew about the Hinkle part—" Just saying *Hinkle* made me lose it all over again.

Augie glared at me murderously. Then he called to his aunt, "Yeah, it's Wyatt. He thought he got bit by a yellow jacket." Looking at me he added loudly, *"But he's okay now."*

Augie stood so that his body blocked me from his aunt's view, while I struggled to my feet and tried to, as my mother would say, "wipe that smile off my face." *Whew.* Okay. Good.

At last, I turned and, with what I hoped was a normal expression, said, "Hello, Mrs. Hinkle."

"Why, hello there, Wyatt. Please, call me Aunt Hilda, won't you?"

I nodded and smiled.

"I was hoping Augie would bring you by one of these days. You boys are in luck. I've been baking this morning."

Wow. Like Augie had said, I'd met Aunt Hilda before. But how was it possible that I had never noticed that she had . . .

"Why don't you boys come on in and have a glass of milk and some nice, warm—"

. . . really, really big . . .

"—snickerdoodles?"

I mean, they were humongous. Like she had two big water balloons under her blue-and-white-flowered shirt. I knew it wasn't polite to stare, especially since she was Augie's aunt and all, so I tried not to.

We followed Aunt Hilda inside and sat down at the round table in the kitchen. Everything happened pretty much the way Augie had said it would. As I was discovering that snickerdoodles are German sugar cookies with a real good cinnamony flavor, Augie asked if he could use the bathroom.

While he was gone I heard a few loud thumps that

sounded like they might be coming from the attic, and I nearly had a heart attack, but Aunt Hilda didn't seem to notice. She was too busy asking me about how I liked being here for the summer with my dad, and didn't I miss my mother, and all those questions people ask when your parents are divorced that are probably meant to be nice, but feel kind of nosy.

I considered for a minute breaking down in sobs about how tough it is for a poor child of divorce like me, in the hope that she would sweep me to her in a warm, comforting embrace, just to see what it would feel like.

But instead I told her I really liked coming here, that I was used to it because I'd been doing it since I was eight, and that I talked to my mom every Sunday. All true and, I could have added, no big deal.

Finally, I thought I heard the front door open, then close, and Augie reappeared and gave me a crazy smile and the thumbs-up sign. We quickly finished our glasses of milk, thanked Aunt Hilda, and left, promising to come back in a couple of days for brownies.

After that, we hid behind a shed until we saw Aunt Hilda go out to the backyard to hang laundry. Augie raced to the bushes out front, grabbed Herkimer, and threw him in the basket on his bike, and we pedaled away like mad.

When we got back to the fallen log where we'd hidden the pellet gun, I took a good look at Herkimer. He was a great horned owl. I knew this from all my trips to the Natural History Museum with Mom. And he was a beauty. His striped body feathers were smooth and soft, and his ear tufts stood straight up. His stern, yellow glass eyes stared so fiercely that I almost felt like he could see me.

"Man, look at his feet!" I said, moving aside the feathers to expose huge, sharp talons. I held him up as if he were flying right at Augie's face and hollered, "Look out! He's coming after you!"

Augie ducked out of the way and said, "Knock it off, Wyatt. Unk will kill me if anything happens to that owl."

"Okay, okay," I said. "So what do we do now?"

"We put Herkimer right here, like so," Augie said as he balanced the mounted owl on top of a fence post. After making sure Herkimer was solidly placed, he picked up the pellet gun and told me to get the boxes of ammo. "Now, you and I hide over here in these bushes so the crows can't see us, and we call them."

I laughed. "What? You know their names?"

I was kidding around, but Augie scowled and said, "No, dummy, we go like this—" and he began to make harsh cawing noises which, I had to admit, sounded pretty cool.

I tried it, and Augie winced. "You'll get better," he said, though he sounded kind of doubtful.

We took up our positions under the bushes, making sure we couldn't be seen from above, and started cawing our heads off. After several minutes I whispered to Augie, "Are you sure about this?"

"I've done it a million times," he answered. "Sometimes it takes a while. There's crows everywhere. They'll hear us soon."

We continued cawing. Suddenly we heard a loud, high-pitched "*Screee-eeeeeee!*"

"There's one!" I whispered excitedly.

"That's not a crow," said Augie. "And stay still!"

"*Screeee-eee!*"

"What is it?"

"I dunno. Maybe it's J.R. and Morrie making fun of us 'cause of our lame crow calls."

I hoped not. J.R. and Morrie were thirteen, two years older than us, and they were major jerks. They seemed to think it was their mission in life to torture us.

They'd swiped our bikes one day when we were swimming at the reservoir. We found the bikes later, ditched by the side of the road. Another time, they'd tripped me when Augie and I were leaving the ice cream stand, and my cone hit the sidewalk. They thought that was hilarious. We pretty much just tried to stay away from them.

"How 'bout if you keep quiet for a while and just let me call," Augie suggested.

"Geez," I said. "I didn't think I was that bad."

Augie looked at me.

"Okay," I said grudgingly. "I'll keep quiet."

Augie was about to give another call when we heard it again, louder this time, and closer.

"*SCREEEEEE-EEEEEEE!*"

Then, from out of nowhere it seemed, a bird—bigger than a crow but not as big as the owl—dive-bombed from the air and attacked Herkimer! There was a *whack* and a flurry of feathers as Herkimer was knocked from his perch on the fence post to the ground.

The dive-bomber flew off with another piercing "*SCREEEEEEE-EEEEEEEE!*"

Augie and I looked at each other in disbelief, then jumped up and ran over to Herkimer, whose severed head lay several feet away from his body.

"Holy moly," I said. Augie had found Jesus that spring and had given up swearing, so I was trying hard not to. "What *was* that thing?"

Augie looked as if he was about to cry. "Red-tailed hawk," he answered. After a minute he added, "I guess they don't like owls, either."

2

We ended up hiding Herkimer's body and head in Bertha's trunk. Bertha was an ancient Buick that sat in rusty splendor up on cinder blocks in the driveway of the house where Augie lived with his grandmother. His grandmother, who he called Gram and who insisted I call her the same, was convinced that Buick was going to be worth big bucks someday.

Augie had tried plenty of times to tell her that just being old didn't make a car valuable. "Gram, if Bertha was in mint condition and had been stored in a temperature-controlled garage all these years, maybe she'd be worth something. But you might as well have Mr. Juliano haul that old rust bucket off to his junkyard."

"Now, Augie, people go crazy for antiques these days! The older something is, the more they like it. Call something vintage and the price quadruples come tourist season, that's Alfred Soames's opinion, and he ought to know," she would say. "You just wait. Bertha is going to put you through college."

Augie had never said it to her because I think he was afraid it would break her heart, but he had told me, "The only way I'm ever going to college is if I grow three and a half feet and magically learn to play basketball, or if they start giving out brain transplants."

I didn't know how to answer that, so I didn't. For me, going to college is kind of like a fact of life, or something. I mean, my parents—both of them actually agree on this—just seem to expect it. My friends at home are planning on it, too, in a way-off-in-the-future kind of way. We all say stuff like, "After college, I'm going to blah blah blah." Nobody ever actually asked me if I *wanted* to go. I guess I do.

But it's different with Augie. I don't really know the whole story about his parents. I think they both just left, but not together. He's lived with his grandmother as long as I've known him. Augie's plenty smart, but I guess he doesn't do so hot in school. There's school smart, and there's Augie smart. Augie knows how to call crows and shoot rats, which we did one night last summer at the dump.

And he knows how to build forts. We'd been talking all summer about making a fort. Now there were only two weeks left before I had to go home, and we were finally going to start that afternoon.

"What are we going to make it from?" I asked as Augie and I rode our bikes down his gravel driveway.

"Not sure yet," he answered. "That's why we're heading to Juliano's."

"I thought that was for junked cars," I said.

"It is, mostly. But Al's got all kinds of stuff there. Some stuff he lets me have for free."

"Let's hope so," I said. "'Cause I'm broke until Saturday."

"What happens Saturday?"

"I get my weekly allowance."

"How much?"

"Ten dollars if I don't have to be told to do my chores. Five dollars if Dad has to say something."

"So what's it going to be?" Augie asked.

"Five," I answered glumly.

"Tough luck," said Augie. "But at least you've got some dough coming."

"Mom gave me a little emergency money, too," I added.

Up ahead I could see the faded and peeling sign that read *Juliano's Metal and Auto Parts—If we don't have it, you don't need it!* Augie and I turned in and I saw his Uncle Heindel and another old guy sitting on lawn chairs outside of a building that said *Office*. There was an upside-down orange crate between them, holding two beers and a checkerboard.

"I figured Unk would be here," Augie said in a hushed voice. "Don't say anything about Herkimer."

I shot him a look as if to say, *Do you think I'm stupid?* Then I whispered back, "But what are we going to do about the . . . you know . . . head?"

Augie shrugged. "We'll fix it later."

I nodded. That sounded like a good plan. If anybody would know how to recapitate a stuffed owl, it was Augie.

"Hey, Al," Augie called as we pulled up to the lawn chairs. "Hey, Unk."

Al said, "Here comes trouble," but you could tell he didn't really mean it.

Augie's uncle said, "Augie, help me out here. This shyster is trying to cheat me."

"How do you cheat at checkers?" Augie asked.

"By making up rules," Uncle Heindel said indignantly. "He claims if he brings a king back to my starting line, I have to king him *again*."

"Huh? Like put a third checker on top of it?" Augie asked.

"Yes! Have you ever heard anything so crazy in your life?"

"So, then what?" Augie asked. "Does that king have, like, superpowers or something?"

"Exactly!" cried Al. "You see?" he said, turning triumphantly to Heindel. "That triple-decker sucker can go forward, backward, *and* sideways. And if you bring him back to get kinged *again*, he can go off the black if he wants to and onto the red!"

I had been standing back, just listening, but I couldn't help blurting out, "But why would he? There aren't any other players on red."

Al turned to me, scowled, and said very slowly, "That's not the point. The point is, he can do it—*if he wants to*." He raised his hands, palms up, and appealed to everyone. "That's the whole point of being a king, right? You can do whatever you want, no matter how stupid it is. Wise or foolish, you're the king!"

I shrugged, trying to stay out of it. I didn't want to

get on the wrong side of Augie's uncle, but we were there to mooch stuff off Al, so it was important not to make him mad, either.

I figured that's what Augie was thinking, too, because he said, "You can't argue with that. I mean, the king is the king."

"Told ya!" Al crowed.

Uncle Heindel shook his head. "I can't believe you'd do me this way, Augie," he said mournfully. "My own flesh and blood . . ."

Al, happy now, said, "So what can I do for you boys?" Turning to me, he added, "And who are you, if I might ask?"

"Wyatt Jones."

"Oh, right," said Al, nodding. "You and your dad are renting a place from Gloria DeMuth."

"Yeah."

To Unk, Al said, "Gloria's kid's the one everybody says burned down my shed." He pointed to an empty space at the far end of the gravel parking lot, where I could see on the ground the charred remains of what must have been a little storage building.

Unk nodded. "How ya doing, Wyatt? It's good to see you."

"Good to see you, too, sir."

"Did you hear that?" Al said with a big smile. " '*Sir.*' I like this kid."

Augie's uncle looked at me and rolled his eyes. "You can call *him* sir, if you want." He pointed to himself. "Me, I'm Unk."

"So I wonder: To what do we owe the honor of this visit?" Al asked.

"Wyatt and me are gonna build a fort," said Augie. "Mind if we look around?"

Al waved his arms expansively. "Look all you want." After a pause he pointed to his right and added with disgust, "Check over there. My sign says *Metal and Auto Parts*, right? But every Sunday when I'm closed, some jokers show up and dump off whatever they want to get rid of. Mattresses, armchairs, a sailboat . . . you wouldn't believe."

Augie and I headed over to where Al had pointed. Tossed in the gravel outside the chain-link fence around the property were a bunch of metal sinks and counters and those big refrigerator things with spigots that serve soft ice cream, some overturned plastic tables and chairs, and some big, messy stacks of wooden siding.

I looked at the wood and then looked at Augie. "It's pink," I said.

"Yeah," he said glumly.

"We can't build a fort out of pink wood." I might be a city kid, but even I knew that.

"Yeah," said Augie. "It would be perfect if only it wasn't—"

"Pink," I finished helpfully.

"Hey, Al," Augie called. "This wood is pink."

"Hey, Augie," Al called back. "No kidding. It's from that custard place they tore down on old Route 9." He laughed. "Like I wasn't going to be able to figure out who dumped it here."

"But, Al," said Augie, "we're building a fort."

"So what?"

"The wood is pink," Augie said.

"Again: So what?" Al replied. "It's *free*. And I hear real men aren't afraid of pink." He guffawed at his little joke. "You can even take the old sign, make the place real classy." This cracked him up even more.

I looked next to the stacks of wood, where there was a big metal frame with metal letters that used to hold light bulbs. The sign read *The Pink Palace*.

I groaned.

But Augie was looking thoughtful. "Gram always says we've got to make do with what we've got," he said. "I guess we could build the fort with the pink on the inside. Then nobody would see it."

"But," I objected, "*we'll* see it. We're the ones who are going to be in it. And a fort is supposed to be a place where you can, you know, hang out and feel great and *relax*, right? I don't know about you, but I don't think I could relax in a pink fort."

Augie considered this. "I see what you mean. But— I know! How about we put up one board with the pink side out and the next one with the pink side in?"

"That's even worse!" I said.

"Yeah, I guess."

We were quiet for a while.

"Why the long faces, boys?" Unk hollered.

"The pink," Augie answered, with a shrug. "It's a problem."

"Haven't you ever heard of paint?" Unk asked.

"Well, yeah," said Augie. "But we don't have any."

"What have I been doing for the past thirty-five years?" Unk demanded.

Augie frowned. "Uh . . . you were the custodian at the garment plant?"

"That's right," said Al. "He was there for thirty-five years, wrestling with that old furnace, trying to keep the women warm."

"That's what I did eight hours of the day," Unk went on. "But what did I do every other waking moment?"

"Um, I don't know," said Augie.

"I painted, that's what," Unk said emphatically. "The minute I finished the bedroom, your Aunt Hilda would decide the living room needed 'a little face-lift.' Then it was on to the kitchen. Then the basement, for cripes' sake. It never stopped. As soon as I finished one room, she'd decide it made another room look 'shabby.' "

Augie and I just looked at him, not knowing what to say.

"My *point* here," he said, patiently, "is that I have paint. Every crazy color you can imagine. I got Aubergine, Mushroom, Avocado . . . or how about Moonglow or Fig Leaf?"

"Do you have any normal colors?" I asked. "You know, like brown?"

"I bet if you mixed all that crap together, you'd get brown," suggested Al.

"I bet you're right," I said.

"Definitely worth a try," Augie agreed.

"Go see your aunt," said Unk. "Tell her I said you can have anything you want."

"Really?" asked Augie.

"Believe me, I'd be very happy to never see another can of paint."

Augie and I headed for our bikes.

"It's all in the basement," Unk called after us. "Which you'll notice is a lovely shade of Spring Cactus with Lime Sorbet trim."

When Aunt Hilda answered the door, I again tried but did not succeed in not looking at her bosoms. When we gave her Unk's message, she directed us to the basement.

"Man," I said, looking around. "Your uncle wasn't kidding."

There were homemade shelves covering one whole wall, filled with gallons of paint, rollers, rolling pans, brushes, spattered tarps—the works. Luckily, we didn't have to go by the weird names they give to paint colors because the cans had all been partially used, and dried paint drips showed on the side of each one.

Aunt Hilda seemed to favor Easter egg colors, including one that could have been called Pink Palace. We avoided those. Finally, we each picked two cans that looked likely. I took a rolling pan and roller, and Augie grabbed a couple of brushes.

Aunt Hilda fussed about how we would be able to carry it all on our bikes, but we put the brushes and roller in my basket and the pan in Augie's, and hung a paint can from each handlebar. Calling "Thanks, Aunt Hilda!" we started off.

If you've never ridden a bike with a paint can hanging from each handlebar, let me just say that it isn't easy. Actually, it's pretty much impossible. With every turn of the pedals, my knee crashed into a paint can—"Ow!"—causing me to jerk sideways, causing my other knee to crash into the other paint can—"Ow!"—back and forth—"Ow! Ow! Ow!"—and throwing me all off balance. I was lurching and wobbling along, feeling like a real dork, hoping nobody was watching, especially J.R. and Morrie, when I noticed Augie was having the same problems. I stopped and stood straddling my bike.

"This is stupid," I called to him. "I don't know about you, but I'm walking."

Augie, looking relieved, got off his bike, too. We

stood for a minute, looking at each other. Then I cracked up. After a few seconds, Augie did, too.

We began pushing our bikes down the road, laughing our heads off, Augie imitating my cries: "Ow! Ow! Ow!"

It took us about a half hour to get to my house, where we wolfed down some peanut butter sandwiches and milk. Dad wasn't home during the weekdays. He was teaching summer classes at the local college. We had a rule that I was to be home for dinner on the nights Dad was home, home by dark on the nights he taught the late class.

Dad was cool that way, so different from Mom. She'd freak if she knew how Augie and I ran around doing pretty much whatever we wanted. It wasn't like we did anything bad. But Mom would want to know *where* and *when* and *are there any adults home* and *did you put on sunscreen?*

Dad said a boy needed a little room and he trusted me to use common sense. He didn't even make me carry a cell phone. He called them electronic nannies, and said kids shouldn't be plugged into gadgets all the time. "How are you going to learn to think for yourself if you call me every time something happens?" he asked.

So I'd only used my cell to phone Mom on Sunday

nights. She probably thought Dad was checking on me a couple of times a day, like she did, but that wasn't Dad's way. He often said things like, "Maybe this ought to be our little secret, eh, Wyatt?"

We bungeed a cardboard carton onto the rack behind the seat on the back of my bike and put the paint cans into that for the ride back to the junkyard. Al gave us a screwdriver to pry off the tops of the cans, and we started mixing. We ended up with a pretty decent sort of muddy color, which Unk immediately named Duck Droppings.

3

We made pretty quick progress painting. There were twelve boards lying in the gravel yard, drying quickly in the sun, when Augie straightened up for a second to stretch his back. He looked at the boards that were left and the remaining contents of the rolling pan and said, "I think we have a problem."

I paused and looked at him.

"Not enough paint," he explained, gesturing at the stack of pink boards.

I examined the situation and set down my brush with a sigh. "You're right," I agreed. "We're not going to make it."

"We could go back to Unk's and get more, I guess," Augie suggested. He didn't look thrilled at the prospect.

"Man," I said dejectedly. "I figured by now we'd have the fort half-built. If we stop to get more paint, the whole day will be gone before we even hammer one nail."

We stared at the ground for a while.

Finally, I said cautiously, "I might have an idea."

Augie looked at me with hope.

"We could just paint squiggles on the rest. You know, like camo."

"*Pink camo?*"

"Pink *and brown*," I said. "The brown would, you know, break up the pink." As soon as I said it, I tried to picture it.

I couldn't.

Then I could.

"Never mind," I said. "Stupid idea."

"Hold on," said Augie. "It might not be as stupid as it sounds." He thought for a minute. "Deer don't see colors," he went on, sounding a little more enthusiastic. "That's why hunters can wear blaze orange. As long as something has a pattern on it, so it blends in with trees and bushes and stuff, it doesn't matter what color it is."

"So, wait. You're saying we don't want *deer* to see the fort?" I asked.

Augie shrugged. "Or anybody else."

"But," I said, "people can see color."

"Well, *duh*," said Augie. "But the human eye can be fooled, you know what I mean? Like one of those crazy pictures where you think you see one thing, but it's really something else?"

"An optical illusion?"

"Exactly! I mean, anybody would see a big pink board out in the middle of the woods, right? But the camo pattern will make it confusing looking, like maybe it's *not* a big pink board. You know what I mean?"

"Kind of," I said, even though I didn't, really.

Augie shrugged again. "I guess it's a dumb idea."

He looked so downcast and sheepish all of a sudden, I wanted to cheer him up.

"No!" I said. "You're right. There's not, like, a *rule* that says camo has to be green and brown. And, anyhow, it'll take forever to get more paint, and I want to get going on this fort."

"Me, too!"

"I mean, we only have two weeks 'til I have to go home."

"Let's do it!"

We started painting like mad, me with a brush, Augie with a roller, making squiggly lines and crazy, random patterns.

"This is a lot more fun, anyway," I said.

"Totally," Augie agreed.

Al and Unk had been playing checkers all afternoon, arguing about the best breed of hunting dog (Al favored the pointing breeds, Unk the coonhound), the right way to grill bratwurst (Al said 'til they bust open, Unk said you had to take them off *just before* they bust open, so they stay juicy), and the correct method for dealing with a skunk living under your porch.

While they agreed that a skunk under the porch was a very delicate situation, Al maintained there was no good solution. "Face it," he said. "You're doomed. Ya just gotta live with the stink until the skunk decides to go somewhere else."

Unk said he knew a guy who had success using a live-catch trap baited with cat food. "But ya gotta use a small trap," Unk warned, "so it can't lift its tail. It can only blast you if it can lift its tail."

I'd been only half listening to them all afternoon, but this was a new and interesting piece of information.

"So *then* what do you do?" I asked. "Once you got a live skunk in a trap?"

Unk shrugged. "The guy didn't tell me the rest of the story."

Al snorted. "Here's the rest of the story: the guy opens the trap, the skunk comes out, lifts its tail, unloads on the guy, and runs back under the porch."

This amused him so much I thought he was going to choke, but he finally recovered and took a swallow of beer. Then he held up the can and shook it. "Empty," he announced. He looked at Unk. "You?"

Unk drained his can and stood up, and the two of them headed into the office, I guessed to get more beers.

Augie and I kept painting. Suddenly he groaned quietly and murmured, "Oh, man. Don't look now, but Morrie and J.R. are coming."

Of course I looked. Sure enough, the two older kids were riding down the road toward us on their bikes.

"They already spotted us," I whispered.

"Hey, look!" called Morrie. "It's Lame and Lamer!"

"Looks like Wimpy and Wimpier to me," said J.R.

They pedaled hard toward us, then braked suddenly, purposely spraying us with gravel and dust from their rear tires.

"Aww, look at that pretty pink wood," said J.R.

"Whatcha making, girls?" Morrie asked.

"Nothing," said Augie, without looking up from his painting.

I admired how casual and nonchalant he sounded. Meanwhile, I stood frozen, not wanting to call any attention to myself.

"Looks like a lot of work for *nothing*," J.R. observed. So quickly I never saw it coming, he grabbed the brush from my hand and dropped it on the ground.

Morrie, seeing this, lunged for Augie's roller, but Augie held on tight. They struggled for a moment, but Morrie was bigger and stronger than Augie. He twisted Augie's arm so the paint-covered foam end of the roller mushed up against Augie's cheek, leaving a big brown streak. Then the roller, too, hit the ground.

"Ew, gross," said Morrie. "What ya been eating, Augie? It's all over your face."

J.R. snickered. "Looks like—"

He didn't finish, because suddenly Al and Unk were standing right there. They moved pretty fast and sneaky for two old guys.

Al looked a little bit like somebody you wouldn't want to mess with, with his bulk and his sudden, fierce scowl. But Unk was pretty scrawny. And, in his plaid hat and yellow-and-red-checked Bermuda shorts, with black socks and giant beige sneakers at the ends of his spindly white legs, he didn't exactly inspire fear.

"This here is private property," Al said, his arms folded over his substantial stomach. "And this is a private party."

J.R. and Morrie tried to cover their surprise at seeing Al and Unk. "Like we'd want to come to your loser party," Morrie murmured, just loud enough so Augie and I could hear it, but not Al.

"So," said Al, "the two of ya—make like a tree and leave."

Morrie looked at J.R. and smirked. "Ooh, I'm scared, J.R. How 'bout you?"

J.R. pretended to shiver with fear. "Petrified." He gestured toward Unk. " 'Specially of him."

They both laughed, but they got on their bikes. As they rode away, Morrie looked back over his shoulder and called, "Sorry we can't stay and play, girls, but you have fun with your pink boards."

The four of us stood there for a minute. I was mad. And, for some reason, I felt kind of embarrassed and ashamed. Which didn't really make sense, since Morrie and J.R. were the ones who had acted like jerks.

Almost as if he'd heard me, Augie shouted, "Jerks!"

"Guys like that," Al said with a shrug. "Coupla punks. Don't let 'em get to you."

"Sooner or later," Unk said, "they'll come up against the wrong people. They'll pay."

I wasn't so sure about that, but I hoped it was true. And if it was . . . boy, did I wish those people could somehow be Augie and me.

But how? J.R. and Morrie were bigger, stronger, and older than us. They were on the football team. I wasn't a major nerd or anything, but I was better at geometry and chess and computers than I was at sports.

Glumly, Augie picked up the roller and I got the brush. We walked over to the office and rinsed off the dirt and gravel, and Augie wet his hands and scrubbed at his face. I wasn't used to seeing him all down like that, and it made me think what a drag it must be to have to live near Morrie and J.R. all year round, not just for the summer.

"Hey," I said, to get his mind off those guys. "Let's finish up this painting fast. While it's drying, we can go to the woods and scout out a good place for the fort."

"Yeah," Augie said. "Maybe we can even get some boards up."

I nodded. We made a quick job of the rest of the lumber, then cleaned up all the painting supplies.

"Just put everything in my car," Unk said gloomily.

"I'd tell you to throw it all out, but lately your aunt's got her eye on the bathroom."

"I hear they got a new color for that," said Al. "It's called You're in Yellow."

With Al's chortles following us down the road, Augie and I headed across a big open field that led to the woods.

Al's junkyard sat on the edge of a big state forest. The forest was named after Ferris Findley, some rich dead guy who used to own it, but Augie and everybody else just called it the woods.

There was an official entrance to the forest on the main road. I'd been there with Dad. There was a lake where you could fish and rent canoes and kayaks, and there were some campsites and trails. But, as Augie had explained to me, hardly anybody ever made it to this side of the forest. There was a really deep gorge right through the middle of the woods. People got there, stopped to look at the gorge and the falls, and turned back.

"So nobody ever comes into the woods this way?" I asked as we approached the trees.

"Nope," Augie said. "There's no road in this way and people don't think of coming through the junkyard."

"Which makes this part of the woods *ours*!" I shouted.

"You bet it does!" Augie shouted back.

We high-fived, then stepped into the woods. After just a short way, it got all dark and shadowy and the air was cooler and piney-smelling. It was real quiet. All we heard was the wind in the tree branches and, once in a while, the chirp of a bird or chatter of a squirrel.

We walked a little farther and came to a stream. It wasn't real big, but too wide to jump over. We dragged over some rocks to make stepping stones, and as we hopped across, Augie said, "Let's pick a spot close to here. I just saw a fish. Plus, it'll be good to be near water."

We walked a little farther, scouting around. "What are we looking for?" I asked.

"Well, with these boards we've got for walls, all we need to do is find some trees just the right distance apart—there!" He gestured excitedly. "See the ones up near the top of that hill? How they grow in sort of a square?"

"Yeah," I said.

"They'll be our four corners."

I took a minute to picture it. "So we nail the boards to the trees to make the walls."

"Right."

"Awesome!"

"It'll be just the right size," said Augie. "Plus, it's far enough in to be secret but not too far to carry all our stuff."

I nodded. Augie was always thinking.

We began lugging boards out to the site. On our final trip, Al gave us a hammer and a coffee can full of nails. First I held up a board and Augie hammered, then we switched. The back wall and the sides went up really fast. We put the squiggly, camo-painted boards on the back wall, so that if anybody *did* come in from the junkyard side of the woods, they'd be less likely to see them.

Then we stopped to admire our work. I couldn't believe how cool it looked already.

"So tomorrow we add the front and the roof . . ." I began.

"And then we stay out here the rest of the summer!" Augie finished.

That was our plan. Since I had to go home in two weeks, we had to make the most of the time we had left. "Have you asked Gram?" I said.

"No," Augie admitted. "But she'll let me if I say

you're allowed. She thinks you're a good influence." He grinned. "Don't ask me why."

I grinned back. "And I'll tell my dad *you're* allowed. He'll go along with it if he thinks Gram said yes."

We bumped fists over this brilliant tactic, and started back to Al's. On the way, I thought I saw a flash of movement out of the corner of my eye, but when I turned to look there was nothing. Probably a squirrel or something. I was going to have to get used to the sights and sounds of the woods, now that it was going to basically be my home for the rest of the summer.

At Al's, the lawn chairs were empty, Al and Unk's game of checkers apparently over for the day. Augie and I got on our bikes and rode home just as it was getting too dark to see, after agreeing to meet up first thing in the morning.

Dad's car wasn't back yet. I put my bike in the shed and was walking to the house when I heard a rustle in the bushes. I stopped to listen. There was another rustle, and another, then someone or something went crashing off through the trees and bushes. It sounded big, as big and clumsy as a bear . . .

Whoa. Bad thought. There *were* bears around. Augie

said so. But he'd never seen one close up. And he said the bears didn't want to mess with people.

Usually.

The noise faded and died away. Whatever it was was gone.

4

I was stoked about the fort and a little spooked by the thing in the yard, so I thought I'd never get to sleep. But I must have crashed pretty fast because I didn't even hear Dad come in.

In the morning, as he and I had a quick breakfast together, I told him about the commotion in the bushes the night before. We went outside, him to get in his car and me to get on my bike, and something caught my eye underneath the bushes at the edge of the gravel driveway, right where the rustling sound had come from. Kneeling down and peering in, I found a rabbit's foot on a silver bead key chain and some gummy worms.

"Look, Dad! Clues!"

"Hmm," said Dad, looking over my shoulder. "I think we can rule out a bear."

"Or a rabbit," I joked.

"This seems like stuff a young kid might have," Dad said thoughtfully.

"Yeah," I agreed. "But what was a little kid doing out so late, hanging around our house?"

"I guess you and Augie have a mystery to solve," said Dad.

"Oh, by the way, Dad," I said casually as he was getting in the car. "Augie and I are building a fort."

"I had a fort when I was about your age. Me and a guy named Chester. We made it out of sheets of roofing tin and a bunch of old oil drums." He smiled and his eyes got a faraway look for a few seconds. "We had some great times . . ."

"Did you sleep out in it?" I asked.

The smile faded. "My parents wouldn't let me. Even though we built it in the vacant lot just on the other side of our neighbors'. Two doors away! What could have happened?" He shook his head at the memory.

I couldn't believe my luck. I mean, I felt bad he never got to sleep out in his fort. But—could there be a more perfect time to ask the big question?

"That stinks, Dad. Augie and I want to sleep out in ours, too," I said.

"Well, it's okay with me," said Dad. "But I'm not

sure what your mother would say, so maybe this ought to be our little secret, eh?"

"Deal," I said.

"When do you think you'll finish?"

"I'm not sure. I think today, but I don't know."

"Where is it?" Dad asked.

"It's right behind Al's junkyard, in the woods."

"Sounds like a good spot," Dad said.

"If we finish today, can I sleep out tonight?" I asked.

Dad hesitated. "I wish I had time for you to show it to me now. But I know the general area you're talking about. Would I be able to find you if I needed to?" he asked.

"Sure," I said. "Just go to the back corner of Al's yard and holler. We'll hear you."

I wasn't sure if this was true or not. I kind of liked to think we were too deep in the woods to hear sounds of civilization. But this was no time to mention it.

I kept talking before he could say no. "Gram's cool with it," I said. Then, figuring it wouldn't hurt to try, I added, "Actually, she said Augie could stay out two nights."

"She did, huh?" said Dad. He gave me a smile that told me that maybe I wasn't fooling him as much as I thought.

"Yeah," I went on. "So we were thinking we'd spend tonight and the next night, and come back early Saturday morning for the weekend."

Dad and I always got our laundry and grocery shopping for the week done on Saturday morning. When all our chores were finished, we did something fun. Last weekend we explored a nearby cavern, which was really cool. Once we hiked a mountain. We've rented kayaks, checked out an airplane museum, stuff like that. When it's rainy, we go to the library or the movies or play board games and cards. Sometimes Augie joins us. Anyway, since Dad had to work all week, weekends were our time together.

"So you'll be home first thing Saturday morning?"

I nodded. "Augie's got chores, too. And church on Sunday."

"Well," said Dad, "I don't see why not. You boys have good heads on your shoulders. And it's not as if you'll be far away. You can always come home if you need something, or if you change your minds."

"Thanks, Dad!" I said. It still amazed me how different he and Mom were about stuff like this.

Dad waved and slowly pulled away, calling, "Have fun."

When he was out of sight, I pumped my fist in victory.

Augie showed up a few minutes later and I gave him the good news.

"We're home free now," he said cheerfully. "Gram thinks your dad's real smart 'cause he teaches college and all. She'll say yes for sure."

I told him about the rustling in the bushes the night before, and showed him the gummy worms. Augie took one look at the key chain and said, "That's Gerard's."

Wow: mystery solved by Augie in two seconds.

"He takes it everywhere," Augie went on. "He kind of rubs it with his thumb. And he loves gummy worms."

Gerard. The name rang a bell, but I couldn't remember why. I guess Augie saw my puzzled expression, because he said, "Gerard DeMuth. The kid whose mom you're renting from. The one who burned down that old shed at Al's." He shrugged. "Or that's what people say, anyway."

"Oh, right," I said.

Dad had said the rabbit's foot and the gummy worms seemed like things that belonged to a little kid, but that description didn't exactly fit Gerard DeMuth. I'd seen him around town before. He had a giant head with a face like a full moon. Once, I'd seen him following his mother around the grocery store, and had been amazed how tall he was. Definitely over six feet. More like six foot seven. And not fat, exactly, but *big*. I remembered thinking there was something kind of weird about him.

"I wonder what he was doing spooking around my house?" I asked nervously. I was glad I hadn't found any matches.

Augie shrugged. "Gram says he's harmless, but she's about the only one who thinks so."

I looked again at the rabbit's foot. I could see where the fur was rubbed thin, probably from Gerard's thumb.

"He loves that thing," Augie said. "I bet he's freaking out about losing it." After a pause he added, "His house is right on the way to Al's. We could stop by, I guess."

"Should I ask him what he was doing last night?"

Augie shrugged again. "You could try."

I was eager to get back to work on the fort. But Gerard's house wasn't out of our way. "Okay. Let's go."

I followed Augie into a short driveway that led to a smallish house painted a bright lavender color Aunt Hilda would probably have loved. You could hardly see the house, though, for all the stuff hanging from the roof's edge: bird feeders, wind chimes, gizmos and doo-dads that twirled and caught the sunlight and made me feel dizzy, a regular flag, a Santa Claus flag, and one with a pumpkin and a witch. In the yard, there were a whole bunch of statues of animals and stuff, and some scraggly flowers planted in tires painted to match the house. It looked pretty crazy, but I got the feeling all those decorations meant a lot to somebody.

We knocked and Gerard's mother answered. "Why, hello, Augie. And Wyatt, is that you?" She looked and sounded tired.

"Hi, Mrs. DeMuth, it's me," I said. "Is Gerard here?"

She looked wary. "Ye-es," she said slowly. "But he's had a bad night, and—"

I held up the rabbit's foot. "I think he lost this."

She broke into a smile that changed her whole face from saggy to happy. "Gerry!" she called. "Gerry! There are some boys here to see you!"

A muffled voice answered cautiously. "Who?"

"Come see, lovey," said his mom. "You're going to be happy, I promise!"

We heard shuffling footsteps and Gerard peered around the corner. His face looked rounder than ever, swollen and red from crying. I'd remembered that he

49

was tall, but he looked gigantic as he came into the small room. His mom looked tiny next to him.

Quickly, I held up the rabbit's foot. Gerard's face underwent a transformation much more dramatic, even, than his mother's. Every bit of sadness disappeared in an instant. His mouth smiled, his eyes smiled, I swear, and his ears and nose and hair were all beaming with what could only be called joy.

I felt like a magician.

Gerard ran over, reached out a chubby white hand, and took the rabbit's foot. He began running his thumb over the smooth fur, talking to it in a low, happy murmur.

I understood then that Gerard *was* sort of like a little kid, even though Augie had said he was somewhere around fifteen or sixteen. His body had gotten bigger and more grown-up looking as the years passed, but his mind hadn't kept up.

There was no way I was going to hassle him about being in my yard the night before, so I looked at Augie and mouthed the words, *Okay, let's go.*

"Glad you got your rabbit's foot back," Augie said to Gerard. "We've got to take off."

"Yeah," I said. "Bye, Gerard."

Mrs. DeMuth walked with us toward the door. "Bless you boys," she said in a low voice. "You have no idea how upset he was . . ." She let the thought trail off. "Sometimes he just wanders away and I—" She paused and said, "I think he's just trying to be like other boys."

I didn't know what to say, so I nodded and Augie said, "Yeah, I know what you mean."

We said goodbye to her and headed out the door. Gerard followed us off the porch and into the yard, happily stroking his rabbit's foot and singing something softly under his breath.

I wasn't really paying attention, but as I climbed on my bike, I thought I caught the words to his little tune. I stopped and listened, holding up a hand to Augie so he'd quit kicking the rusty kickstand on his bike and listen, too.

In the sudden quiet, Gerard's voice rose and fell in a singsongy rhyme:

> "*My name is Gerardo,*
> *I am a retardo.*
> *My name is Gerardo,*
> *I am a retardo . . .*"

I couldn't believe my ears. Gerard was saying a really terrible, mean word, one everyone knew you were never supposed to use. Not about anybody. Ever. And the worst thing was, he was saying it about himself.

"Why are you singing that?" I asked. I guess the question came out louder than I realized, because Gerard stopped singing, looking scared. He backed away, anxiously rubbing the rabbit's foot.

"I didn't mean to yell," I said quickly. "I just wondered . . . where'd you learn that—that song?"

He stopped and smiled once more. "Morrie and J.R. taught me it," he said, adding proudly, "It has my name in it. It's a good song, huh?"

For a few seconds I couldn't speak. I looked at Augie. In his face I could read the same disbelief and anger I was feeling.

"Don't you like it?" Gerard said, sounding distressed. "It has my name in it."

I hesitated, looking at Augie. I knew he was thinking the same thing I was: it was an awful song. But Gerard was so proud of it, it would feel even meaner to ruin his enjoyment.

"Not everybody has a song with their name in it," Augie said, finally.

"But I bet we can come up with an even better one," I said. I didn't really think about this. It just sort of came out. "What do you say, Augie?"

Augie glanced at me uncertainly, but said, "Yeah. Sure."

Gerard looked at us eagerly, as if he expected us to burst out with a new song right there on the spot.

"We're gonna need a little time to come up with something," I said. "Meanwhile, don't sing that one. It is just not good enough to be your song."

Augie shook his head. "No way," he agreed.

"No way," Gerard said, shaking his head.

"Ours will be way cooler," I promised.

Augie nodded.

"Way cooler!" said Gerard happily.

"I mean, Gerardo isn't even your name," I said.

I was thinking it was going to be hard to make up a song about Gerard because I didn't know anything about him, really, except that he liked gummy worms and his rabbit's foot. And fire. But we couldn't let him go around singing that other one.

"Okay, Gerard," said Augie. "We've got to go now."

"Where you going?"

"We're building a fort," I said. Right away, I wished

I hadn't said that. Maybe building a fort was something Gerard had always wanted to do, too, and nobody ever asked him. I felt bad about it as we pedaled away.

But the fort was Augie's and mine.

5

"Can you believe J.R. and Morrie?" I asked Augie
when we were out of Gerard's earshot.

"Jerks," he said. "It's bad enough they torture us,
but picking on a kid like Gerard?" He shook his head
disgustedly.

"Teaching him that song . . . Geez."

"But how are *we* going to make up a better one?"
Augie asked. He sounded a little desperate.

"I don't know," I admitted. "We'll just have to think
of some words that rhyme and put them together, I
guess. I mean, J.R. and Morrie came up with two
crummy lines. We can do better than that."

"If you say so," Augie said. But he sounded doubtful.

"We just have to get in the right mood."

"Okay," he said. "But first—the fort. I was thinking

we'd use a tarp for the roof. But then I was thinking it'd flap around in the wind and probably leak. It would be better if we could get some sheets of tin or something like that."

"Let's ask Al," I suggested. "My dad told me he used roofing tin to build a fort when he was a kid. Maybe we can find some lying around."

When we got to the junkyard, Unk's car wasn't there yet. We found Al sitting in the office at a metal desk, which was covered with piles of grubby papers.

"Come over here and look at this, boys," he said.

Augie and I went around behind the desk and stood next to him. He pointed down at a calendar open to the month of July. "Now this," he said, "this I understand."

There was a picture of a lady wearing a red, white, and blue bikini, a cowgirl hat, and cowgirl boots, standing in the open bed of a red pickup truck. She was holding a flag in one hand and a bottle of STP motor oil in the other.

Augie and I looked, not sure what it was that Al understood, but willing to keep looking.

Then Al flipped past August, September, October, and November, and Augie and I caught quick glimpses of other ladies leaning against cars or getting in or out of cars, or pumping gas into cars, none of them wearing much. He stopped at December and said, "But *this*? This I don't understand at all."

He pointed a greasy, stubby finger at the picture of a lady wearing a very small red bikini decorated with white fur, a Santa Claus hat, and white furry boots. She was standing by the open door of a car in about six inches of snow, holding a bottle of STP motor oil with a big red bow tied around it. She was smiling like mad, like standing around freezing to death in a bathing suit was about the most fun she'd ever had in her life.

It was so dumb, Augie and I both laughed. I figured Al was thinking the same thing we were.

But he said, "Boys, that right there is a 1957 Ford Thunderbird convertible, with the original Colonial White paint job, white *leather* seats, tricked out with white-walled tires and custom chrome hubcaps!"

Augie and I looked at him in surprise. I didn't know about Augie, but I hadn't noticed the car so much.

Al put the calendar back down on the desk with a thump, sending papers flying in all directions. "Now I ask you," he said, "what in the name of your great-grandmother's girdle is that girl doing taking a car like that out in December with the ice and snow and all the lousy drivers, not to mention the salt they put on the roads? I mean, you gotta ask yourself, is she *crazy*?"

I had to admit Al had a point, even if it wasn't the first one to come to mind.

"Totally nuts," I said.

"Insane," Augie agreed.

Al tossed the calendar toward the overfilled wastebasket in the corner. It fell to the floor and he waved at it dismissively.

"So," he said, "you kids gonna work on your clubhouse today?"

"Fort," Augie corrected him. "Yeah. We got the sides up and we were wondering, are there any sheets of tin roofing or anything like that out in the yard?"

Al tilted his head back and closed his eyes. I figured he was going over every corner of the junkyard in his mind. After a while he sat up and opened his eyes. "I think there's something you can use leaning against the fence on the southwest side."

Augie looked at me. "Let's go!"

As we headed for the door Al said, "Ya might wanna park your bikes behind the office here from now on. Keep those two jamokes Morrie and J.R. from seein' 'em and bothering you."

"Good idea," I said.

"Yeah. Thanks, Al," said Augie.

As I followed Augie out the door, I watched him dip smoothly and, with one hand, pick up the calendar from the floor.

What did I say before? Augie's always thinking.

"Score!" I said as we moved our bikes.

Augie grinned, rolling up the calendar and putting it in the basket on his handlebars. "Gotta have something to read in the fort besides comics, right?"

"Totally," I agreed.

Al's voice came booming from the office. "And don't think I didn't see ya swipe that calendar, smart guy."

We wandered around Al's yard. It was interesting. I hadn't figured a junkyard would be organized, but it was. There was a section full of all different kinds of vehicles: a hearse, a Good Humor ice cream truck, a school bus, an ambulance, and a rusty old hippie van painted with peace signs. Along the wall nearby were washing machines, refrigerators, and all kinds of appliances. There was a whole area devoted to wheels: car, truck, tractor, and steering wheels.

I started over to check out some pinball machines and arcade games, but Augie said, "Over here, Wyatt!"

I walked past a car that looked like it had come from a fun house ride. It was sitting all alone, surrounded by weeds, its bright paint faded and peeling. I wanted to check it out, but Augie was pointing excitedly at a stack of corrugated metal sheets piled against the fence.

"Wow," I said, "all we need is two or three of those babies, and we'll have a roof!"

"You bet," said Augie. "So that just leaves the front. We could build walls and a door somehow, I guess."

"Yeah," I said slowly, trying to picture how we'd do it. I had no clue, but probably Augie did.

"Or we could use a tarp for a flap," he said.

"That sounds quicker," I said.

"Yeah," said Augie. "Come on, let's each grab a piece of this metal."

We started dragging the metal sheets toward the entrance to the yard. They were pretty thin, so they weren't heavy. But each one looked to be about eight feet long and four feet wide, so it got kind of tricky maneuvering them through all the junk. Plus, we had to be careful handling the edges, which were really sharp.

When we finally got back to Al's office, Unk had

arrived, and he and Al were setting up their checker-board and chairs outside.

"Okay if we take these?" Augie asked Al.

"Be my guest," said Al.

"And I took some rope," Augie added. "Is that okay?"

"Sure."

"Oh, and do you have any tarps?"

"For cryin' out loud," said Al, "what do I look like, a junk dealer?" Then he banged his palm against his forehead. "Oh, yeah, I forgot for a second there. I *am* a junk dealer!"

This amused him so much it took him a while to re-cover. "Tarps," he gasped at last. "I think they're all being used. But, hey, ya want a tarp, ask a painter." He gestured to Unk.

"Oh, yeah," said Unk, rolling his eyes. "I got tarps. All sizes and shapes. Plastic, canvas, vinyl, you name it."

"Awesome," said Augie. "Could we have one? I mean, borrow one? We'll bring it back at the end of the summer."

Unk echoed Al. "Be my guest. Go see your aunt. I think she's making brownies today."

We decided to get the roof materials out to the fort

first. It was even tougher dragging the sheets of tin through the woods than it had been moving them out of the junkyard. They kept getting hung up on the underbrush and low branches.

When we got to the fort and eyeballed the roofing material next to the wall, we saw we would need two more sheets, so we headed back to Al's.

As we were struggling along with our final haul, I felt the metal slipping from my sweaty grasp. I adjusted my hand to get a better grip, and felt a burning pain as the metal sliced open my palm near the base of my thumb.

Somehow I remembered, for Augie's sake, not to swear. Dropping the tin, I hollered, *"Mama mia! Ay, caramba!!!! Pasta fazool!!"*

I was vaguely aware of Augie laughing hysterically as I sucked away the blood to get a better look. Immediately, I felt like puking. I was looking at the *inside* of my hand, like the *guts* of my hand, the stuff that's supposed to be inside the skin and out of sight because it is really, totally disgusting and gross.

Augie must have seen my face, because he got to his feet with a look of concern.

"Sorry, Wyatt," he said, getting hold of himself. "Are y'okay?"

"Yeah," I said, but I heard my voice coming out kind of wobbly.

"Is it bad?" Augie asked. "Should we go have Gram look at it?"

I hesitated. "I don't think so." I wasn't sure, really. But we were so close to finishing the fort. We *had* to have our first sleep-out that night. "I just need something to stop the bleeding."

Augie looked down at his T-shirt. "This thing is really old," he said, and ripped off a strip from around the bottom. Pointing to my wound, he said, "Let me see that."

I held out my hand and he wrapped the cloth around it several times, going around my thumb to leave it free. Then he tucked in the end. It was a pretty neat job, and it didn't hurt too much. Mostly I was just glad I didn't have to look at it anymore.

Using a little extra care, we got the rest of the tin to the fort. Augie sized up the situation and said we needed to add boards to the front walls to make them a little higher than in the back, so we did that. Then we laid a final board across the front and back to make a ceiling beam. We hoisted up the sheets of tin, and overlapped them so they'd fit, and so the edges wouldn't leak. If it rained, the water would run downhill in the corrugated ridges and off the back.

"Genius," I said.

We nailed the edges of the roof to keep it from blowing away, then went to get the tarp at Unk's.

Aunt Hilda was kneeling on the ground weeding her garden when we got there. She waved and we went over. I was holding my hand behind my back so she wouldn't see it, because if she was anything like my mom, she'd make a ginormous stink about it and want to do the whole first-aid thing, or even drag me to the hospital.

Augie told her what Unk had said about borrowing a tarp.

"My hands are all filthy," she said, waving them in the air so we could see. "You boys go on in and help yourselves to brownies and milk, and take any tarp you like."

Inside, as we ate, I said, "Too bad we didn't bring that owl. We could sneak him back to the attic, no problem."

"Yeah, no problem except for him not having a head," Augie replied.

"Yeah. What are we going to do about that?"

"I'm thinking superglue," Augie said confidently.

I wasn't convinced that superglue was going to work, but I didn't say anything. Maybe he was right. I hoped so.

On the way out, I forgot about hiding my hand. Some blood had seeped through the T-shirt bandage and Aunt Hilda spotted it.

"Wyatt, what on earth happened to you? Come over here and let me see that hand of yours."

Augie and I exchanged a look, but there was no way out of it.

"It's not too bad," I said.

She hustled us right back inside, asking a million questions about what had happened, and was the metal rusty ("a little"), and had I had a tetanus shot (I had no idea but said, "Oh, yes.").

Aunt Hilda washed her hands at the kitchen sink and came back from the bathroom with her arms full of bandages, gauze, special little scissors, and a bottle of what I really hoped wasn't alcohol, but was.

She unwrapped the strip of T-shirt, scolding all the while about how it wasn't a proper bandage, but in a nice way. She picked up the alcohol and a gauze pad. Then she moved in very, very close, and bent her head down. Her giant bosoms were poking out over the top of her V-neck shirt, right in front of my eyes. They looked like two soft pillows nestled in there.

"This is going to sting, Wyatt, so you'll need to be very brave. Think about something else for a minute."

She leaned even farther forward to get a closer look at my hand.

"Something that makes you happy," she went on.

No problem there.

"Are you ready?" she asked.

"Not quite," I said, thinking my happy thoughts.

"Now?" she asked.

"I guess so," I said.

It was over much too soon.

When she'd finished disinfecting, Aunt Hilda examined the cut and decided I didn't require stitches. Next she applied a bandage she called a butterfly, which would hold the two sides of open flesh in place so they could heal together. Then she wrapped gauze over that, taped it in place, and patted my hand with a warm smile.

Dazed and nearly speechless, I managed to thank her. She sent us on our way with the rest of the brownies wrapped in foil.

Back at the fort, we tucked the tarp under the tin

along the front edge. Then we positioned it so it hung almost to the ground and nailed it in place. Augie hammered a couple of big spikes into the front roof board and attached a piece of rope to each one. We rolled up the tarp and tied it there.

"If it's raining or we're doing something, you know, top secret, we just undo the ropes and—" Augie demonstrated and the flap fell.

I crawled underneath it into the fort. "It's really dark in here with that down," I called. "We're going to need flashlights."

Augie rolled up the flap. "It'll probably be up most of the time," he said. "But, yeah, we definitely need lights."

Occasionally munching on Aunt Hilda's brownies, we spent the rest of the day riding back and forth from our houses to Al's, where we piled our supplies: sleeping bags, flashlights, cards, comics, a couple of fishing poles, and matches in a little baggie to keep them dry. Gram gave us some old enamel plates and cups, silverware, a superheavy cast iron frying pan, an empty gallon milk jug, and some duct tape. I asked about those last two things, but Augie said he'd show me later.

At my house we got food: a jar of peanut butter, a

loaf of bread, granola bars, Slim Jims, two bags of Oreos (the world's best cookie, we both agreed), cheese sticks, some apples and pears, a bag of red licorice sticks (my personal favorite—Augie likes black better, but we didn't have any), and some bottles of pop and water.

Augie rummaged in the refrigerator and took out a plastic tub of margarine.

"Do you think your dad would mind if we take this?" he asked.

"I doubt it," I said. "What for?"

"For frying stuff."

I looked at our collection of food. I'd never had fried Slim Jims before but, now that I thought about it, I bet they would taste pretty good.

Augie grabbed some salt and pepper and added it to the pile. We put it all in our backpacks.

I wrote a note for Dad and left it on the kitchen counter. I took the rest of the notepad and some pens, and put them in my backpack, too.

"What's that for?" Augie asked.

"Writing down ideas for a song for Gerard."

Augie nodded solemnly. "Excellent."

All day long we had kept our eyes peeled for J.R. and

Morrie. On the way back to Al's, we had a pretty close call. I spied them getting on their bikes in front of a convenience store near Augie's house and called to Augie, "J.R. and Morrie ahead. Take evasive action!"

We turned down a side street and pedaled away without them seeing us. We bumped fists as we rode side by side.

By then it was around four o'clock in the afternoon, and we were finally ready to start taking stuff out to the woods.

Al and Unk had been watching with great interest as the pile grew, and had made some useful suggestions and a few contributions, like two lawn chairs even more beat-up than the ones they were sitting on and two orange crates to use as a table and a shelf.

"Ya want to take this, too," Al said, unrolling a small square of old linoleum and displaying it for us to see.

"What for?" asked Augie.

"Ya ever slept on the ground before?"

"Not really," we both admitted.

"Yeah, well, I have," Al declared. "It's hard. And damp. Put this down. You'll thank me tonight."

We thanked him right then.

Unk, who had been listening, remarked, "That joint gets any fancier, I might ask can I move in."

By the time we were about to haul our last load out to the fort, it was close to six o'clock. Al and Unk were packing up for the night. We stored our bikes out of sight inside the fence, and Al locked up.

"Have fun, boys," Unk said.

"Yeah," said Al. "Have fun. And if you hear some really bloodcurdling screams tonight—like somebody's getting their heart ripped out by a wild animal while they're still alive?—don't worry about it. I hear stuff all the time when I'm here late, and I don't believe those old stories for a minute."

Augie and I looked at each other.

"Old stories?" I repeated.

"What old stories?" Augie asked.

Unk broke in then. "Now, Al, don't go trying to scare these boys."

"Who's trying to scare 'em?" Al protested indignantly. "Didn't I just say if you hear something horrible, don't worry about it?"

Don't worry about it?

"Pay no attention to this joker," said Unk. "Just go—and have a good time."

Augie and I started walking toward the woods. Behind us we could hear Al laughing and Unk scolding him.

"He was messing with us, right?" I asked.

"Totally," said Augie.

"He made the whole thing up," I said.

"I never heard any stories like that."

"Nothing to worry about."

"Heck, no."

We were quiet for a while. I don't know about Augie, but all I could think about was not thinking about what Al had said.

Augie got us back on track.

"Dude," he said, "we're about to camp out in the most awesome fort ever!"

"Darn right!" I said.

When we reached the fort, we dropped the stuff we were carrying.

I stretched my back and said, "What do we do now?"

"How about we get some squirrels for dinner?" Augie asked.

"Heck, yeah!" I said. I'd never hunted squirrels before. Or eaten one. But now we were really getting down to it. This was *exactly* the kind of thing I'd imagined you did when you had a fort. "How do we get 'em?"

Augie reached into one of the giant pockets on his cargo shorts and took out a slingshot. "Meet the Squirrel-Slayer."

"No way!" I said. "You've actually gotten squirrels with that thing?"

"Sure," Augie said. "Ask Gram."

I didn't have to ask Gram. If Augie said he'd sling-shotted squirrels, I believed him.

"Let me see that," I said.

Augie tossed it to me and I checked it out. It was a Y-shaped stick with thick rubber strips going from the tips of the Y to a leather pouch. "Did you *make* this?" I asked.

"Yeah," he said, sounding surprised. "They're thirty-four bucks at the store."

"Does it really shoot?"

Augie grinned. "Shoots good."

I'm telling you. That Augie.

Then I thought of something. "Why don't we use your pellet gun?"

Augie shrugged. "Too easy."

"For you maybe," I said. "So, anyway, what do squirrels taste like?"

"Good. Like squirrel."

"How do we get 'em?"

"First," said Augie, "we need ammo." He leaned down and picked up a small roundish pebble.

We continued walking, eyes on the ground, occasionally picking up a pebble with the right shape and pocketing it.

"We should probably hurry," Augie said, glancing up at the sun. "Squirrels are out in the daytime, not at night. Let's hope they're getting ready to have a little snack before they turn in."

He led the way to some pine trees and found a pinecone. "See how a squirrel's been eating the nuts out of this? They love these things. We just have to be still and hope he comes back—with a few of his buddies."

We crawled under some low-hanging branches and sat.

"We gotta stay *really* still," Augie whispered. "We may have to wait awhile, so get comfortable. If you see one, whisper to me. Don't stare at it, just kind of look at it out of the corner of your eye."

73

He got out the slingshot, pulled back the pouch, and tested his aim. Still whispering, he said, "Squirrels always pull the same trick. They run around to the side of the tree and freeze there where you can't see 'em. So hang on to this." He handed me a stone, about twice as big as the one in the pouch of his slingshot. "When I tell you to, chuck it to the other side of the tree."

"Okay," I whispered back.

We sat there, still and quiet as anything. I'd never really just sat in the woods like that, and it was pretty cool until a bunch of little flies started buzzing around my face. One landed on my nose. I wanted to swat it in the worst way. Augie must have read my mind because he hissed, "Stay still!"

I sat as quietly as I could, remembering a movie I saw where Indians buried a guy all except his head, and ants came and crawled all over his face, and he couldn't brush them away or anything, since his arms were buried. But he wanted to prove to the Indians he was tough, so he never twitched, even though they were *biting* ants.

Next thing I knew, a line of ants was crawling on *me*! And even though my arms were free, Augie had said I couldn't move. So I watched as they trooped right over my outstretched leg, like that was their usual route and whatever this thing was that was in the way wasn't going to stop them from following it. They didn't bite, but they did tickle like crazy.

It seemed like a long time went by. Then I heard a rustle. Something was coming our way through the dead needles on the ground! Then it stopped. Then, scamper, scamper, scamper. Stop. Scamper, scamper, scamper. Stop. I slanted my eyes in that direction and, sure enough, there was a squirrel, sitting up on its hind legs, eyes darting everywhere, nose sniffing like mad. Then scamper, scamper, scamper, and jump! It leaped into the pine tree and quickly ran around to the other side of the trunk, out of sight, just the way Augie had said it would.

My heart was pounding like crazy. I slid my eyes toward Augie and lifted my eyebrows in a question: *Now?*

Augie raised the slingshot into position, gave me a little grin, and nodded.

I threw the rock so it landed on the other side of the pine tree. I guess the squirrel thought we'd moved and could see it now, so it ran around to our side of the trunk.

Augie let the stone fly—and the squirrel dropped to the ground and was still.

I couldn't believe it. It was like Augie was some kind of squirrel wizard or something, or like he had made a robot squirrel that did exactly what he told it to do!

"*Wooo-hoooo!*" I shouted.

We got to our feet and went over to examine the squirrel. It looked kind of peaceful, like it was sleeping.

I examined its long bushy tail, its little clawed feet, and its rounded ears, and pushed open its mouth to see what kind of teeth it had.

"Wow, check these out!" I said, showing Augie the four long, sharp front teeth, two on the bottom and two on the top. "They're orange!"

"Weird, huh? Like a beaver's," said Augie. "If you keep one for a pet, you have to trim those teeth or they just keep on growing."

This was interesting. "Really? Forever?"

Augie nodded.

"So, like, the teeth would just grow right up into its brain?" I said.

"Yup," Augie said cheerfully.

"And the top ones would turn into giant fangs?"

"Yup."

I was picturing that when Augie handed me the slingshot. "Your turn."

"Okay." I'd never even held a slingshot before, forget about shooting a squirrel with one. But it had looked pretty easy when Augie did it—not that I'd actually seen what he did, it had been so quick.

So we sat back down in our same positions, only Augie had the chucking rock and I had the slingshot.

It seemed to take longer this time, and I was beginning to get restless and my stomach was growling so loud I figured every squirrel in the woods could hear it, when suddenly I heard the same scamper, scamper, scamper. Stop! Scamper, scamper, scamper. Stop! A squirrel was rummaging around on the ground. It found a pinecone, held it in its paws, pulled off the scales, and started chomping on the nuts.

I looked at Augie out of the corner of my eye. Was I supposed to shoot now or wait until it went up the tree? Augie nodded and moved his lips soundlessly. *Now.*

I had slowly slumped down while we were waiting, so I had to kind of wiggle up to get in position.

The squirrel froze.

I froze.

After a long time, the squirrel began munching again, only it looked nervous.

I raised the slingshot, real sneaky-like, and pulled

back the pouch. It was harder to pull than I'd expected, and the Y part started wobbling as I tried to figure out how to aim.

The squirrel turned and, I swear, it frowned at me for a few seconds. Then it was gone. Too late, my stone flew and landed about four feet away, nowhere near where the squirrel had been.

"Geez," I said. "That stunk."

Augie shrugged, putting the slingshot in his pocket and picking up his squirrel by its tail. "No sweat. You know how many times I've shot this thing? Come on. We'll clean this at the stream."

We? I thought.

Luckily, Augie cleaned while I watched. He took a pocketknife, cut off the tail, and then made a few more careful cuts. Then he tugged a few times and it was like he slipped the critter out of its fur coat, slick as a whistle. Then he pulled out the guts.

The squirrel looked oddly human now. "It kind of looks like a pygmy," I said. "A dead pygmy. A naked, headless, armless, footless pygmy," I added.

Augie laughed and started cutting the body into pieces for frying. He nodded toward the skin and guts. "Why don't you bury those over there someplace."

"Sure. Hey," I said, holding up the tail. "Maybe I'll keep this." I was picturing attaching it to my bike's handlebar, or to the back of a baseball hat, or even— "Hey, we could fly it from the fort, like a flag!"

"We could," said Augie. "We'd have to boil it and salt it, though. Or it'll start to stink."

"Oh. Yeah. Like with mummies, right? Didn't they use salt on them?"

Augie shrugged.

I decided to bury the tail. I didn't have a shovel, and digging a hole with a stick didn't work so great. Then I spotted a fairly big rock half-buried in the ground and got an idea. I pried it up, dropped the tail and the pelt and the guts into the hole it left, and covered it back up—sort of—with the rock.

At the fort, we got set up. There were leaves and twigs on the ground inside the fort, and we brushed them out the doorway, and threw out all the rocks we could feel. Then we laid out Al's linoleum, which was a little small, but covered a good part of the ground. When we'd spread out our sleeping bags and set up the orange crates with our other stuff, the place looked great.

Then we gathered wood, cleared an area in front of

the fort, and started a fire, which was easy with all the dry pine needles and twigs around.

Augie took the empty gallon milk jug and a cup and headed toward the stream. When he came back, I saw he'd filled the jug with water, which seemed like a good idea what with the blazing fire and all.

When the flames died down a little, we put two big rocks on either side of the fire and balanced the frying pan on top. I threw in a gob of margarine. When it was sizzling, Augie put in the pieces of meat and I sprinkled salt and pepper on them.

The smell of the frying meat was incredible.

We ate some cheese sticks while we stared hungrily at the pan, turning the pieces of meat from time to time.

When I was about to die of starvation, Augie declared the meat done.

We sat in the drifting smoke from the fire, gnawing squirrel meat off the bones and slathering slices of bread with margarine.

"What'd I tell you?" Augie asked.

"You said it would be *good*," I answered.

He looked at me, surprised. "You don't like it?" He shrugged. "Oh, well. More for me, then." He reached over and grabbed the remaining two pieces from the pan.

"Not so fast!" I said, taking one of them back. "You said it would be *good*. But *this* . . . this is *epic*. This is the best meal I've ever had in my whole life. *The. Best. Ever.*" I stuffed a whole slice of bread in my mouth for emphasis.

Augie grinned. "Yeah? I mean, you've been to some real fancy restaurants, right?"

I nodded, but repeated with my mouth full, "Uh. Beft. Eh-er." This cracked us both up, and when I laughed my whole mouthful of bread kind of shot out right at Augie. He threw it back at me, and I picked it up and finished it.

We chewed every shred of meat off the bones, licked our fingers clean, and finished it all off with some Oreos and licorice.

The nice white bandage Aunt Hilda had wrapped around my thumb was pretty dirty from all the work we'd done and greasy now, too, so I pulled it off and threw it into the fire. The cut had some dried blood on it, and still hurt a little, but not much.

It had gotten pretty dark by then, so we piled more wood on the fire, and Augie got out the calendar he'd swiped from Al.

Even with the fire built up, it was kind of hard to see.

Augie got a flashlight and rummaged around for a minute. He came back with the milk jug filled with water and the duct tape, and pressed the lit end of the flashlight against the side of the jug.

"Hold this here while I tape it," he told me.

The beam of light shining through the jug made the whole thing glow—"Like a lantern!" I said. "So *that's* why you brought that stuff."

"Gram and I do this whenever the power goes out," Augie explained. "Which happens a lot."

I sat back and admired the lantern. It seemed to me that Augie knew how to do everything—everything important, anyway. For a second, the question popped into my head: What am *I* good at? No answer came to mind. I shrugged the thought away.

We sat by the fire, going through the calendar, month by month, examining the pictures by the light of the lantern. There was a lot to discuss. One thing we agreed on for sure was that when we were old enough to drive, we were going to own pickup trucks.

When the fire died down we doused the embers until they were cold, then got ready for bed. We left the flap open and lay back on our sleeping bags, looking out at the stars shining through the tree branches and shooting the breeze. After a while we grew quiet.

"I wish we could live out here all the time," I said.

"Mmm," said Augie.

I could tell Augie was just about asleep, and so was I. But I fought to stay awake, thinking how this was the best night of my life and I didn't want to miss any of it.

6

It was great waking up in the fort, with the whole day and another whole night ahead of us. It was at that moment when I realized the real beauty of a fort. There's nobody to tell you what to do or when to do it.

I felt my hand throbbing a little, so I held it up to have a look. There was just enough early morning light coming through the trees so I could see. It looked okay. I remembered Aunt Hilda asking if I'd had a tetanus shot. I'd said yes, but I had no idea, really.

Suddenly a book I'd read popped into my head. It was about some old-time explorers who were trying to find a river in Canada. They got totally lost and ended up spending the winter, which they didn't plan to do, and they all died of starvation and cold, except for the guy who lived to write the book. And one of them got cut with a dirty knife and got tetanus, except in the book they mostly called it lockjaw.

The book included gruesome, detailed descriptions of all the guys dying. The author really got into telling about the guy with tetanus: how his body spazzed uncontrollably, his neck muscles got all stiff, and how he died with a horrible grin frozen on his face because his jaws clenched tight and wouldn't move.

Thinking about all this gave me an idea for a terrific trick to play on Augie.

I waited until he started squirming around in his sleeping bag, making little noises like he was starting to wake up, and I let out a loud moan.

Augie squirmed some more and rolled over onto his back, eyes closed.

I moaned again.

"Mmmmmm," said Augie. "Whazzzat?"

I moaned louder and longer.

Augie suddenly shot up to a sitting position, looking around in confusion. "What's that?" he cried. "What's going on?"

I tightened my face into a horrible frozen grin, just the way I imagined the guy from the book looked.

Keeping my neck stiff, I twitched in a series of shivery spasms. From between clenched teeth, I managed to gasp, "Ock-aw."

Augie stared at me in dismay. "What's the matter with you, Wyatt?" he said.

I made the whole length of my body go spazz again, and stared up at Augie all wild-eyed and crazed.

"I can't—" he said. "What are you—are you sick?"

I held up my injured hand. "Et-us. Um a ut. *Ock-aw.*"

"Wyatt, can't you talk normal? I can't understand you! What the heck is the matter with you?"

"Ock-aw!"

Augie looked at me, a mix of horror and frustration on his face.

I spazzed again, then pointed weakly toward the notepad and pen which I had set on the orange crate shelf the night before. Augie jumped to his feet, grabbed them, and handed them to me. Keeping the upper half of my body and my face rigid, I took the pen, held it in a clawlike grip, and wrote, shakily, *Lockjaw.*

Augie stared at the word, his own jaw dropping.

Dying, I added.

Augie's eyes bugged. "*What? No! Don't die!* Wait!" He stood stock-still for a second, clearly trying to think. "What should I do? Should I go for help?" He nodded. "Yes! You—stay right there! *But don't die!* I'll be right back and—"

I couldn't keep it together any longer. Watching Augie freaking out was just too much. I started shaking with silent laughter. At first Augie looked at me with even deeper concern, no doubt worried that I was entering my final death throes.

Then, when he realized that I was actually laughing—hysterically—at him, he fell to his knees and started pummeling me with his fists. He wasn't really hitting me hard, and I was partly protected by the sleeping bag, so it barely even hurt.

"I wish—" I said, gasping for air between bursts of laughter, "you could—have seen—your face!" In a high, shrill voice I cried, *"Don't die! You can't die!"*

"You're gonna die, all right, you little twerp," said Augie furiously, grabbing both my arms and holding them. "Right now!"

I grinned the horrible frozen grin at him and said, *"Ock-aw!! Ock-aw!!!"*

At this, Augie cracked up, too, and we both rolled around for a while until we were able to get hold of ourselves.

So, all in all, it was a pretty great way to start out our second day.

7

We lazed around for a while, then we dug for worms and headed to the creek with our fishing poles. Most of the stream was pretty shallow, but we walked until we found a place where some big boulders and a fallen tree had made a deep pool. We snuck up close.

"Try this," Augie whispered. I watched him cast onto the bank right near the edge of the water, then twitch the tip of his pole enough to make the worm drop in.

Bam! A hungry little brook trout flashed out of nowhere and grabbed the worm. Augie flipped the fish up onto the bank.

Then he took a piece of fishing line from his pocket and made a stringer, looping one end through the trout's mouth and gill, tying the other end to his belt loop.

That way, the fish stayed cool in the water but couldn't escape.

Neat.

"Okay, so first we'll catch the little guys hanging out near shore," he explained. "Then we'll keep casting farther out, and finally we'll see if there's any big ones hanging out in the middle, at the bottom of the pool."

"Genius," I said.

"Go easy," Augie warned, "so we don't spook them."

The plan worked great. We caught a bunch of little fish, then some bigger ones, and then Augie got a ginormous one. They were beauties, with red and yellow spots and some blue spots on their sides, and I was feeling kind of bad when they died until Augie started talking about how great they were going to taste.

We built a dam with rocks and made a little pond to keep the fish cool until we cooked them. Then we swam and goofed around in the water and didn't get out until we were all shivery and pruney.

We lay around by the side of the stream, drying off and warming up in the sun.

"I'm starving," I said, suddenly realizing I was.

"Me, too," said Augie.

He showed me how to clean the fish and we took

turns, using Augie's pocketknife. It was no big deal: you just cut off the head, make a slit up the belly, and scoop the guts out with your finger. Augie said it was okay to put the guts back in the stream for crayfish and stuff to eat. We went back to the fort, built the fire up, waited for it to settle down some, then heated up a glob of margarine. When it was sizzling, we put in the fish. Augie said the skin was one of the best parts, but you had to let it get really crispy.

It was hard to wait, I can tell you.

I think maybe those fish were even better than the squirrel. We crunched right into the little ones, eating them whole, tiny bones and all. We ate the meat off the bigger ones, pulling the skeletons out and throwing them on the fire.

We finished off our feast with cookies and just sat for a while, feeling full and lazy.

"This is the life," I said.

"Definitely," Augie agreed.

When we got tired of sitting around, we went to check out the gorge. We had to hike a long way through the woods. We could hear the waterfall before we saw it. Looking over the edge at the steep, sharp drop, I could see why nobody ever came across from the other side.

We walked upstream for a long while, to a place where the cliffs weren't quite so steep. Augie said he'd heard about people finding fossils in the cliffs, so we searched around. Neither of us had ever found a fossil before. We figured we'd know one when we saw it, but if we did see one, we didn't know it.

By the time we headed back, it was starting to get dark. We had just crossed the little stream near our fort when I noticed that the rock I'd used to cover up the remains of the squirrel had been moved. I called Augie over.

"Look," I said, pointing. "That's where I buried the stuff. Do you think an animal found it? Like a raccoon or a bear?" The idea of a bear being so close to where we'd been sleeping the night before was both exciting and scary.

Augie examined the hole and the overturned rock. "Where's the tail?" he asked, looking perplexed.

I looked again. "It's gone!"

We stared for a minute.

I said, "That is *so* weird. I mean, most animals would be after those nice stinky guts, right?"

"Right," said Augie thoughtfully. "It's definitely weird that it only took the tail. There's not much meat on a tail."

We looked at each other.

"Weird," I repeated.

"*Definitely* weird."

Augie kicked the rock back over the remaining stuff, and we went to the fort, picking up firewood on the way.

Once we had the fire going, I was rummaging around in the semidark to find the peanut butter and bread when my fingers closed on a squishy little plastic baggie. I held it up to the light from the fire.

"What the—?"

Augie glanced over and frowned. "I don't remember bringing those," he said.

"We didn't," I answered.

The bag was filled with gummy worms.

"Gerard," we both said together.

"*Gerard* was *here*?" I said. It hardly seemed possible. "What was he doing here? This is *our* fort. It's supposed to be *secret*."

Augie was still staring at the baggie.

"Is anything missing?" I asked. I found a flashlight and began to look around.

"What I can't figure out," Augie said slowly, "is whether he was sneaking around, and he dropped the gummy worms by mistake . . ."

"Yeah?" I said. "Or what?"

"Or, I don't know, maybe he left them on purpose."

"What? Like a warning? *I'll be back to burn down your fort?*"

"Maybe like a . . . I don't know . . . a *present,*" said Augie.

"I don't even like gummy worms," I said. "And why would he give us a present anyhow?"

Augie shrugged.

"It gives me the creeps to think of somebody else being here," I said.

"I know what you mean," Augie agreed.

We sat quietly for a while, looking out at the night. I didn't know how to describe it, but it felt like something perfect had been ruined somehow. I tried to shake the feeling as Augie and I made peanut butter sandwiches and ate them by the firelight.

We played poker for matches. I creamed Augie, and after that I felt a lot better.

I woke up several times during the night, my heart pounding, expecting to see Gerard's big, white moon face staring in at me. But nothing happened.

8

In the morning, we headed home.

"See ya Monday," I told Augie.

"Yep. I'll come over early," he said.

Dad and I finished our usual Saturday grocery shopping and laundry by noon. We spent the rest of the day at the county fair, staying late for the fireworks. Sunday it rained, so we went to the movies and fooled around at home, playing poker, five-card draw. He was teaching me all about odds and betting and bluffing.

We'd been playing pretty even. It was my deal, and I gave myself two jacks, which I held. Dad held four cards and threw in just one. I dealt his card, then gave myself three. I got two nines and another jack, meaning I had—*yes!*—a full house. I tried to maintain my poker face, but it wasn't easy.

Dad examined his hand and bet three matches. I saw

his three matches and raised him two. He saw my two and raised two more.

Uh-oh. Was I overplaying my hand? No! I didn't think so, anyway. I raised two more.

Dad threw in two more matches. "Okay, hotshot," he said. "This is getting too rich for me. I see you and call you."

I laid down my full house. Dad groaned and put down a queen-high flush in clubs, a pretty decent hand.

"Read 'em and weep!" I said, something I'd learned from watching movies. I made a big show of hauling in all the matches. "Are you sure you want to keep playing?" I teased. "Your match pile is looking a little, uh, *low*."

"It's considered bad form to gloat when you win," Dad observed.

"Sorry. I couldn't help it."

"It's getting late. You'd better give your mom a call."

"Oh, right. I forgot."

After we'd talked for a while, I asked Mom, very casually, if I'd had a tetanus shot. Pranking Augie about having lockjaw had been fun, but I didn't want to be sick for real. Immediately, I wished I'd never brought it up. Mom asked me a million questions and made me put Dad on to make sure I didn't need an ambulance or something. Anyway, the good news was, I did have the shot.

Monday morning, Augie and I met up to head back out to the fort. The plan, approved by both Dad and Gram, was that we could stay there until dinnertime Wednesday. Then we had to come home for a night to "get re-civilized," as Gram put it.

Augie came to my house and we loaded up our backpacks with supplies. Dad had helped me pick out stuff that doesn't spoil, like cans of tuna fish, beef jerky, saltines, nuts, dried fruit, granola bars, and a new tub of margarine. He'd also let me get junk food like potato chips and Cheetos, which we didn't usually buy, but he winked and said he'd heard they went well with squirrel. I'd spent part of my allowance on extra flashlight batteries.

"Good score," Augie said approvingly. He had two new comics to contribute, as well as some homemade cookies from Gram, some tomatoes from her garden, and marbles for the slingshot. We planned to hunt squirrels again.

Al and Unk weren't there yet when we stopped to stash our bikes at the junkyard. We headed straight for the fort. As we crossed the stream, we saw right away that the rock was overturned again. This time, the squirrel skin and innards had been disturbed. Actually, they were gone.

Augie and I looked at each other.

"I guess maybe it *was* an animal before," I said uncertainly.

"I guess maybe," Augie agreed.

But when we got to the fort, the flap was hanging crookedly, half-open. And when we looked inside, it was obvious right away that someone had been there again.

First, we were hit with a horrible smell that almost made me toss my breakfast.

We hadn't exactly cleaned up on Saturday morning, but we'd left our sleeping bags rolled in one corner and our other stuff in the orange crate shelf or on the table. Now our cards and comics were thrown all around. There was a heap of blackened stubs, as if somebody had lit one match after another and watched them burn down.

The smell came from the remains of the squirrel, which sat in a disgusting, stinky pile on top of one of the sleeping bags—which just happened to be *mine*. Worst of all, the whole pile looked like it was moving, which was really creepy. Then I realized it *was* moving—crawling with maggots, actually—which was *way* creepier.

"Oh, man!" I said. "Gross!"

I picked up the sleeping bag—making sure not to touch anywhere near the maggots—and took it outside, where I gave it a good shake, sending the guts and maggots flying. I probably should have walked farther away from the fort, but I just wanted that stuff *off my sleeping bag*.

Going back into the fort, I looked around again. "What the heck?" I said. "I can't believe he came back."

Augie looked as freaked out as I was. "I just don't get why he did this."

I pointed to the matches. "From what you've said about him being a firebug, I guess we're lucky he didn't burn the place down. I never should have told him we were making a fort."

"You didn't tell him to come here and trash the place," said Augie.

"*Man.* We were nice to him! We offered to make up a new song for him!"

We were quiet for a minute, trying to take it all in. Then Augie said suddenly, "The calendar!"

We looked, but it was gone.

That did it.

"Let's go," I said.

At the same time Augie said, "He's toast."

9

Quickly, Augie and I stashed our supplies, pulled the flap down, and hurried back through the woods.

Al and Unk were setting up their table and chairs when we reached the junkyard.

"Did you see Gerard around here this weekend?" Augie asked.

Al held up his hands, palms out. "Whoa there! No 'Hi, Al, how ya doin'?' What's got your panties in such a bunch?"

"Sorry," said Augie. "Hi, Al. Hi, Unk."

"That's better," said Al with a smile.

"So what's up?" said Unk.

"Gerard's been at our fort," Augie explained. "Messing things up and taking stuff."

"The DeMuth kid?" Unk asked.

We nodded.

"Well, if that don't beat all," said Unk, shaking his head. "First he burns down Al's shed. Now this."

"Hey, I'm willing to give him the benefit of the doubt in regards to the shed, ya know? I mean, I got no proof says it was him. And, truth be told, I had no use for that dilapidated old heap of boards. *But*," he declared, "a man doesn't mess with another man's fort. It's just not done. A guy's fort is his *castle*. It's—what do you call it?—*sacred*."

We all nodded.

"So what are ya gonna do?" Al asked.

"Go to his house," I said, getting on my bike.

"Careful now," Unk called after us as we rode away. "That kid's kind of funny in the head, you know. He's big, too. There's no telling what he might do."

We found Gerard in a lawn chair in his front yard, petting what looked like a little gray kitten sitting on his knees. We ditched our bikes and walked up to him, and as we got closer, I saw that it wasn't a kitten after all.

"Augie!" I said in a low voice. "He's got the squirrel tail."

The tail was spread across Gerard's knees and he was running his chubby white fingers down the furry length of it, over and over again. In his other hand, his thumb rubbed back and forth over the rabbit's foot.

101

Gerard looked up then, saw us, and grinned, like he didn't have a care in the world. He didn't even look guilty, which really bugged me.

"Where did you get that?" I asked, pointing to his lap.

His grin faltered for a second, but then returned big as ever. "Want to feel it?" He held out the tail. "It's real soft. Soft as a rabbit."

"What were you doing in the woods?" Augie asked, ignoring Gerard's outstretched hand.

"Wait a second," I said. Something was bugging me about seeing Gerard with the squirrel tail, besides the obvious fact that he'd found it right near our fort. "Augie, didn't you say that thing would stink after a while?"

"Huh?" said Augie, looking surprised by my sudden changing of the subject. "Oh. Yeah." He thought for a minute. "It *oughtta* stink by now."

I didn't feel like getting close enough to find out for myself, especially after almost upchucking from the guts in the tent, so I asked Gerard, "Does it? Does that squirrel smell bad?"

Gerard shook his head. "My mom called it nasty.

She was going to throw it away. But Gerard said no! So she fixed it."

Fixed it? This was interesting. I wanted to ask how, but Augie was looking impatient. I figured she must have done that boiling-salting thing that Augie had told me about.

"Gerard, we know where you found that," he said. "What were you doing in the woods?"

Gerard pointed to me. "*You* said. Remember? You said you were making a fort."

"So you followed us?" I demanded.

He nodded. "You saw me," he said, and—I swear—he giggled, like it was a secret little joke.

I had a brain flash of that brief second in the woods when I thought I'd seen something out of the corner of my eye, then had dismissed the idea.

It must have been Gerard.

"I like the fort," Gerard went on. "It's nice. But there were no gummy worms."

"Yeah," I said. "We saw your gummy worms. They were almost as nice as the squirrel guts on my sleeping bag."

"And you took our calendar!" said Augie.

"What were you doing lighting all those matches?" I added.

Gerard's eyes popped open, and he looked very frightened. "Gerard does *not* play with matches!" he cried.

"Then why did you?" I asked.

"No! Not Gerard!" he blubbered, beginning to cry. His hands rose from his lap and fluttered nervously. "No matches for Gerard. No matches! No fire!" His round white face had turned bright red, and his eyes kept on blinking really fast.

"Come on, Gerard," I said. "You admitted you were there. Just give us the calendar, okay?"

"And promise you won't go back," Augie said.

At that, Gerard did this weird thing where his eyes rolled up and to the side, almost like he was trying to disappear, or like he thought if he couldn't see us, maybe *we'd* disappear. He became very still. His hands, which had been stroking the rabbit's foot and squirrel tail, froze. He was like a big, blind stone statue.

I looked over at Augie and we stared at each other, wide-eyed, wondering, *What do we do now?*

I thought for a minute. Gerard had been in the woods, for sure. He had the squirrel tail to prove it.

He'd been in the fort for sure, too: he'd left the gummy worms. But, for some reason, I believed him about the matches. And if he hadn't lit them and trashed the place and taken the calendar, who had?

I was pretty sure I knew.

I said, "Okay, Gerard. You're not allowed to play with matches. You promised you wouldn't. And you didn't, did you?"

Gerard's face relaxed. His eyes opened and darted from mine to Augie's and back as he shook his head no. He looked down happily at the squirrel tail and the rabbit's foot and his hands began their rhythmic stroking again.

"So who *did* light the matches?" I went on.

The eyes flew up under the lids again and stayed there. The hands froze. The statue was back.

"Do you know?"

No answer.

I tried a different tactic, trying to get him to relax. "Was it your mother?" I asked in a teasing voice.

Gerard's eyes flew open. "No!" he said, and laughed as if this was the funniest idea in the world.

"Was it Augie's gram?" I tried.

"No!" he said, laughing even harder.

I laughed, too, and said, "Okay, now I'll ask for real: Was it J.R. and Morrie?"

Gerard's eyes flew back in his head and he was still again, except for his lips and hands, which were trembling.

I glanced at Augie and nodded. He nodded back. Then he said, real slowly and quietly, "It's okay, Gerard."

There was no answer from the statue, but I thought the trembling eased up a little.

"We're not mad at you," I said. "I just wonder how those guys found the fort."

Gerard opened his eyes. In a very small voice he said, "They took it and they wouldn't give it back." A little sob escaped from his throat.

"What did they take?" I asked.

He looked down at the squirrel tail in his lap and stroked it fiercely.

"They took your squirrel tail?"

"And they wouldn't give it back!" Gerard said, crying openly. "They wanted me to tell, and they didn't give it back, and they kept asking me—"

The door to the house opened then, and Gerard's mother stepped outside. She smiled at Augie and me and started to say hello, but then she caught sight of Gerard's tear-streaked face.

"Oh, lovey, what's wrong?" she said, rushing over to him. She knelt down and put her arms around Gerard, then turned to Augie and me with fury. "Haven't you boys anything better to do than come around here to torment a poor kid who never did you any harm?"

"I—we—" I started to protest, but Mrs. DeMuth was shepherding Gerard toward the door. She stopped and looked back and, sounding more sad than angry, she said, "I've never seen him so happy as when you took him to that fort of yours. And now look at him! I hope you're proud of yourselves."

She led Gerard inside and the door closed.

Augie and I looked at each other.

"Man," I said.

"Let's go," he said.

"She thinks we took him to the fort," I said as we walked dejectedly to our bikes.

"Yeah," said Augie. "Like he was our friend."

I felt pretty crummy right then, and I could tell Augie did, too. I'd never really thought about what it must be like to be Gerard and not have any friends.

I could just picture what had happened. J.R. and Morrie had seen Gerard playing happily with his new squirrel tail, swiped it, then started to tease him with it: *Where'd you get this, Gerardo? Really, the woods? What were you doing in the woods? Oh, there's a fort there? Those losers Augie and Wyatt made it? Oh yeah? So where is it? No, you can't have the squirrel tail back, not until you tell us . . .*

Before we got on our bikes, Augie and I spit in our palms and shook hands on a solemn vow.

J.R. and Morrie were going down.

10

"We can plan our strategy when we get to headquarters," Augie said as we pedaled next to each other on the way to Al's. "I'm thinking we should call this Operation Doom."

"Yeah!" I said. "Or—hey! How 'bout we call it Operation *Ultimate* Doom?"

"How 'bout Operation Ultimate Doom and Destruction!" Augie came back.

"Perfect," I said. Then I added, "It would be really cool if it made a good acronym."

"Huh?"

"You know, like SCUBA."

Augie looked at me again like, *Huh?*

"SCUBA. It stands for Self-Contained Underwater Breathing Apparatus," I explained. "And POTUS is

President of the United States. And the first lady is FLOTUS."

Augie shook his head. "I never knew what that was called. So, you mean, like SOB is one of those? An ack—"

"Acronym, yeah. But ours would be . . ." I spelled it out: "O-U-D-A-D."

Augie made a face. "How would you even say that? Ow-dad? Sounds like a little kid who got hurt, crying for his father. That's dumb."

"Or Oo-dad."

"Even dumber."

I thought about it. "I bet SCUBA sounded dumb, too, the first time somebody said it. SCUBA, SCUBA, SCUBA."

Then I tried, "OUDAD, OUDAD, OUDAD. See?" I said. "It doesn't sound any dumber than SCUBA."

"Um, Wyatt?" said Augie. "Can we just forget about the acro-whatchamacallit and concentrate on the mission?"

"Okay," I said. "Sure."

We were quiet for a while. My mind had gotten stuck on trying to make up a cool acronym, so I forced myself to think about J.R. and Morrie and the lousy things they'd done. That got me mad all over again. Then, when we got back to the fort and I imagined J.R. and Morrie being there, fooling around with our stuff, I was seriously ticked off.

We built a new fire and sat staring at it.

"You can always think better by a fire," I said.

"Definitely," Augie agreed.

After a minute, I asked, "So, did you think of anything?"

"Not yet."

"Me neither."

A couple more minutes went by.

"Anything?" I asked.

"Nope."

Finally, I offered, "We need something diabolical. Fiendishly clever."

"For sure," Augie agreed.

"Something that'll really teach those jerks a lesson."

"Yeah," said Augie.

"So they'll never mess with us—or Gerard—again."

"Yeah!" said Augie, turning to me for a high five.

After a few more minutes, I said, "Right here: *this* is where it's got to happen. They're definitely going to come back here."

Augie nodded.

"So we need to be ready for them."

"Um-hmm."

"They're older than us," I went on. "And bigger and meaner." I grinned. "But we have the advantage of superior brain power."

Augie grinned back. "Goes without saying."

"Every good military tactic uses the element of surprise," I said. "I read that somewhere, anyway."

"Makes sense," said Augie. "That's a good start."

"And"—an idea hit me—"Gerard should be here to watch it happen."

"Totally," agreed Augie.

We high-fived.

"I'm getting hungry," said Augie.

"Me, too."

"Want to do some squirrel hunting? While we think more, I mean?"

"Might as well," I said.

Augie handed me the Squirrel-Slayer.

"You sure?" I asked. "I mean, we could starve to death before *I* hit one."

Augie handed me a few marbles. "These are easier

112

to aim than stones. You'll see. Take a few practice shots."

I did. I guess I got a better feel for the slingshot, but I didn't actually hit anything I was aiming at. I didn't want to waste Augie's valuable ammo, so I gathered up the marbles and handed them back.

"You shoot, and I'll chuck the rocks," I said. "I need way more practice, and I want to eat *sometime today*."

Augie shrugged, and I returned the slingshot. We found another pine tree full of cones and set up underneath it, the way we had before.

As we sat very still waiting, half of my brain concentrated on listening for squirrels, but I let the other half work on the J.R.-Morrie problem.

When we'd finished, Augie had shot two squirrels, and I still hadn't thought of anything close to a plan.

As we cooked the squirrel meat, we racked our brains.

"I keep coming up against the same problem," I complained.

"What's that?" asked Augie.

"We don't know when J.R. and Morrie will come

back. Like if they came right now, what would we do? Pelt them with hunks of squirrel?"

"Waste of good meat," Augie muttered.

"True," I said. "But we can't let them have the element of surprise."

"I don't think we have to worry about that," said Augie, looking pleased with himself.

"Why not?"

"Because," he replied, wiggling his eyebrows, "I happen to know they have JV football practice every weekday starting today."

"Really?" I said, unable to believe this piece of good luck. "You sure?"

"Yep," said Augie. "They all complain about how hard Coach works them. They only have off on the weekends. I figure they're dying to get back here and cause more trouble. I bet they'll come Friday night. Possibly Saturday or Saturday night."

"Well, that's great except for one thing," I said. "*We* won't be here on Saturday."

"Yeah, I know," said Augie. "So I was thinking . . . if we go home Wednesday night like usual and do all our chores, I bet I can talk Gram into letting me stay here Saturday, and even Sunday if we need to. She won't

be happy if I have to miss church, but"—he shrugged—
"it's worth a shot."

"Yeah," I said. "And if Gram says yes, Dad probably
will, too."

"Cool," said Augie. "So we've got all week to get
ready."

We grinned at each other.

"We'll definitely come up with a plan by Friday,"
I said.

"Definitely," said Augie. "Meanwhile, ya wanna go
find some crayfish?"

"For what?" I asked, wondering if maybe this was
going to be Step One in the new plan Augie was cooking up.

"Bait," he said.

"You want to go *fishing*?"

"Yeah," Augie said.

"What about the plan?"

"We can think while we fish," Augie answered.

I groaned. "I just remembered something. We still
have to come up with a song for Gerard."

"We can think while we fish," Augie repeated.

We found a bunch of crayfish by turning over rocks
at the bottom of the stream. Augie said trout went crazy

for them, and he was right. By the time we'd caught six fish and cleaned them, it was getting dark. So we made a fire and ate, throwing the fish skeletons onto the flames like before.

"Tomorrow," I said sleepily. "Tomorrow we'll come up with a plan."

"And a song," added Augie.

11

In the morning, we decided to go talk the situation over with Al and Unk.

When we got to the junkyard, they were set up at the checkerboard, arguing about who was the best baseball player ever to play the game, Babe Ruth or Willie Mays.

"Bottom line: Ruth had 714 homers, and Mays only had 660. End of story," Al declared.

"Homers-schmomers," Unk shouted. "Mays also had 3,283 hits, 1,903 RBIs, and 338 stolen bases. There's no comparison. End of story." He glanced up, saw us, and looked relieved. "You two, tell him. There's no comparing the Babe and Mays!"

Augie and I looked at each other. Al and Unk could go on about this for hours. But we knew how to get them *really* riled up. It was impossible to resist.

"Forget those old guys," said Augie. "Barry Bonds was the best, hands down. He had 762 home runs."

"Yeah, but Roger Clemens was better than Bonds. Come on, 354 career wins!" I said.

Al and Unk looked at us with outrage, just as we'd known they would.

"Coupla dopers!" Al said with disgust. "They don't even belong in the same conversation we're having here."

Unk shook his head and looked at Augie mournfully. "I never thought I'd see the day when my own nephew would stand up for a couple of low-life cheaters who just about ruined the game. I'm very disappointed, Augie. Very disappointed."

Augie started laughing then, and I did, too. "We're only kidding, Unk," Augie said. "Just trying to yank your chain."

Unk looked relieved, but Al said, "I oughtta give you two bums some calluses on your kiesters." He pretended to glare at us, but I could tell he was enjoying the joke.

"So," Augie said, "here's the deal. It wasn't Gerard who messed with our fort, after all. It was J.R. and

Morrie. And they'll be back, for sure. So we want to be ready for them. Get 'em to back off."

"For good," I added.

Al nodded approvingly. "Gotta do it."

"But we're having trouble figuring out how," I said.

Al thought for a minute. "I have one word for you," he said.

"What's that?" I asked.

He said something, then folded his arms over his stomach, smiling with satisfaction.

"That's two words," I said.

Al held up his hands, palms out, and looked at me with annoyance. "Okay, Mr. Smarty-Guy. Two words."

"Sorry," I said quickly. "What you said—those things, what are they?"

Al looked disgusted. "Kids today don't know nothing," he muttered.

"Easy now, Al," Unk protested. "They're eleven. They never went to 'Nam."

"Yeah, I suppose," Al admitted grudgingly. To Augie and me he said, "Well, don't expect me to spell out everything. Use your noggins. Use that intercom you kids are so crazy about."

I looked at Augie, confused.

Augie grinned. "He means *Internet*," he said in a low voice. "I think."

"Yes," said Unk, his face brightening. "Goggle it! I hear you can find out anything that way."

I was confused again, but only for a second. Then I smiled. "Yeah, Google's awesome."

Augie and I looked at each other.

"Let's go," I said.

"Where?"

"The library."

Augie and I got set up on a computer at the public library and began our search. I spend a lot of time on the computer when I'm home at my mom's and I've gotten pretty good at finding what I want. Dad had insisted that the summer be tech-free: no computer, and cell phones only for emergencies and calling Mom. I'd been afraid I'd go nuts, but Augie and I had been so busy, I hadn't missed that stuff at all. Now, sitting in front of the screen, I got right back into it. I have to admit, it felt kind of good to be better at something than Augie, for a change.

Starting with the tip from Al, we checked out a lot of different sites.

We kept on reading and looking at pictures.

Augie started getting excited. "Hey, we can do this stuff! No problem."

I nodded. I was getting excited, too. Possibilities were already forming in my head. All we'd needed was a nudge in the right direction.

We got some wicked-good ideas. Using a piece of scrap paper and one of those stubby little pencils you only see in libraries, I made a list of things we were going to need.

I filled four pieces of scrap paper with notes.

We finally had the makings of a real plan.

"This is going to *totally* mess with their minds!" said Augie.

"Roger that," I said. I thought the circumstances called for some of the official-sounding military language we'd been reading online. "Our mission is to create panic, fear, and humiliation in the enemy, leading to flight and utter defeat. Of course, we will be aided in this enterprise by the element of complete surprise." I paused and added, "We didn't start this. But we are going to finish it."

Augie looked impressed. "Yeah! Like you said!" He raised his hand and we grinned and high-fived.

The lady at the checkout desk looked over at us and raised an eyebrow, but she smiled when we walked by. "Did you boys find what you needed?" she asked.

"You bet," I said.

12

Augie and I rode to my house, where I got the twenty-five dollars Mom had given me for emergency money. She had warned me not to spend it frivolously, so I'd left it in the little pouch in the main compartment of my suitcase where I wouldn't see it all the time and be tempted.

"But if this isn't an emergency, I don't know what is," I said to Augie, who totally agreed.

I also took a bag of balloons that had been left in one of the drawers in the living room cabinet. Then I opened the refrigerator and held up a package of hot dogs. "In case we're too busy today to go hunting or fishing?" I asked.

"Good thinking," said Augie.

I grabbed some rolls, too.

Then we rode to Cooney's Hardware. My dad was

crazy about the place, so we were there a lot. Dad said it was like hardware stores ought to be, not like Walmart, he said, where you had to buy a plastic-wrapped package of one hundred different-sized screws when you only needed one, and where nobody knew anything about hardware.

We said hi to Mr. Cooney, the owner. He looked about a million years old and shuffled around the store in felt slippers and baggy pants held up by suspenders.

Wooden bins lined the walls, filled with nuts, bolts, nails, hooks, screws—you name it—of every size and shape you could ever want. Rolls of wire and rope leaned against the walls. The middle of the long, narrow room was filled with tables piled high with what looked like a totally random assortment of stuff. Some of it was what you'd expect to see and some of it was weird. All of it was interesting.

"Check this out, Augie," I said, laughing, holding up a bottle of something called Predator Pee. Reading the label, I said, "It's pee from coyotes and foxes. It keeps deer from eating your bushes."

I expected him to laugh, too, and crack a joke. But instead he said, "Aw, you don't have to *buy* that stuff. Gram gets hers from a guy we know."

That Augie. He wasn't kidding. There were about a hundred different questions rushing into my head, beginning with, *You actually know a guy who collects pee?* Followed by, *How the heck does he get it?* I pictured a guy with a bottle in his hand, sneaking around behind a coyote, waiting for just the right second.

I didn't get a chance to ask Augie any more about it, because Mr. Cooney shuffled over then and asked if he could help us.

I took my scribbled notes from my pocket. "Um, we need some of these," I said, pointing to a little sketch I had made.

Mr. Cooney nodded. "Seven-eighths-inch screw eyes. How many?"

I looked at Augie.

"How much are they?" he asked.

"Three cents apiece."

"We'll take thirty," said Augie.

Mr. Cooney nodded again. He headed slowly toward the back wall and, without hesitating, reached for a bin full of just the little doohickeys we wanted. He counted out thirty and put them in a small paper bag.

"What else?"

I showed him another sketch I'd made.

"One-inch screw hooks," said Mr. Cooney, nodding again. "How many?"

"Thirty of these, too, I guess."

After he'd gotten the screw hooks, we went through the rest of the list: a large spool of one-hundred-pound test monofilament fishing line, another large spool of thin metal wire, and a box of heavy-duty rubber bands.

When we left, I had $16.32 left in my pocket.

Next we stopped by Augie's house, where we grabbed a large jar of honey from Gram's pantry. This, too, they got from "a guy we know."

"But this guy keeps *bees* instead of *pees*," I said, and finally got a laugh from Augie.

Next we went to Al's, where Augie asked Unk if he had any old empty paint buckets.

"Heck, Augie, I got about a hundred of 'em. They're out in that shed in the yard, you know where I mean?"

Augie nodded. I knew, too: it was the shed we'd hidden behind when we "borrowed" Herkimer. With everything going on, I'd forgotten all about the owl. An idea tickled the back of my brain.

When Augie asked if we could take some buckets, Unk said, "You'd be doing me a favor. Your aunt's been after me to clean out that shed."

Augie grinned and turned, looking like he was about to hop on his bike and leave.

"Ahum-hmmm," I said, clearing my throat loudly.

Augie kept on walking.

"Ahem," I said, louder this time.

Augie turned to me with a puzzled expression. "What's the matter with you, Wyatt?"

"I hope you're not getting one of those summer colds," said Unk. "They can be a real bear."

I bugged out my eyes at Augie, but he just stared, confused. Obviously, he'd forgotten this part of our plan.

Finally, I said, "Didn't you have something else you wanted to ask your uncle, Augie?"

Augie's face cleared as he remembered. "Oh, yeah. Hey, Unk, does Aunt Hilda have any nightgowns that are, like, you know, kind of see-through? Or—what's the word you said before, Wyatt?"

"Um, flimsy," I said in a low voice, suddenly thinking maybe this hadn't been such a good idea after all.

"Yeah, that's it," said Augie. "Does she?"

He looked expectantly at Unk, whose eyes, I was dismayed to see, had grown narrow. "What kind of smart-aleck question is that?" Unk asked. "Why, I oughtta—" He stopped, his mouth opening and closing like a fish as he tried to think of what he oughtta do to us.

"What'd I say?" Augie asked, looking bewildered.

Al broke in then. "Now, Heinie, settle down a darn second here, will ya?"

Heinie? Had Al really just called Unk *Heinie?* I guess it was the obvious nickname if your parents were clueless enough to call you Heindel. Any other time I'd probably have been rolling on the ground, dying of laughter. But just then I was too nervous.

Al spread his arms, palms to the sky. "Don't you kids know anything? Ya don't ask a guy about his wife's unmentionables! That's why they're called unmentionables: 'cause ya don't mention 'em, ya got it?"

"Aw, Unk," Augie said. He looked crestfallen, a vocabulary word I'd never really understood until that moment. "We didn't mean anything you're not supposed to mention, did we, Wyatt?"

I shook my head.

"It was just part of our plan to prank J.R. and Morrie. But never mind. I didn't know the rule about unmentionables. Just forget it," he pleaded.

Al turned to Unk. "Okay, so they didn't know. Now they do. They didn't mean nothin' by it."

Unk nodded. "All right. It's up to your aunt, anyway," he said. "You go ask her." He added with a weak smile, "Just tell her what you want it for, okay?"

"Sure thing!" Augie said quickly.

"Thanks!" I called as I ran to my bike.

"Man," said Augie as we rode off. "That was weird."

We got to Aunt Hilda's house, and she was happy to give us all the empty paint buckets we wanted. Which were, lucky for us, a lot easier to carry on a bike than full ones. Plus, we each had a cardboard box bungeed on the racks over our rear wheels because of all the stuff we'd been hauling back and forth to the fort.

"If you need more, you know where to find them," she offered. "Now, you said this is part of a trick you're playing on some other boys?"

"J.R. and Morrie," I answered. "Do you know them?"

"Oh, yes," she said. "They're the ones who smash up my nice pumpkin decorations every Halloween. I know boys will be boys, but that just seems so—unnecessary, don't you think?"

"Yes, I do," I said. "Which is why we were wondering if you could help us out with something else?"

"Why, certainly," said Aunt Hilda. A little sparkle showed in her eyes and she winked. "I'd be happy to help you teach those two a lesson. As long as no one's going to get hurt," she added.

"Oh, no," Augie said. "We already decided. No injury. No death. No dismemberment."

Aunt Hilda laughed. "Well, that's a relief. So what can I do?"

Carefully, we explained about the nightgown. Aunt Hilda clapped her hands with delight. "I have just the thing!" she said. "Hang on. I'll run and get it."

She returned, holding up a long white nightgown that was exactly what I'd been picturing. "It's kind of sheer," she said, "but that's what you're going for, right?"

"It's great!" Augie said.

"Perfect," I agreed. But then I had a thought. "Is it, you know, your best, most favorite nightgown or anything? I mean, what if it gets dirty or torn or something?"

"Oh, heavens," said Aunt Hilda. "I'm not worried.

It's been hanging in my closet for ages. I'd forgotten about it. I can't even remember the last time I wore it. I think it was getting a little tight on me."

I looked away from both Aunt Hilda and the night-gown, trying not to picture her and it together, wondering why my imagination came up with stuff like that at the worst possible moments.

Beaming, Augie said, "Thanks, Aunt Hilda."

"Yeah, thanks," I managed to say.

We were on our bikes, almost out of sight of the house, when Aunt Hilda came running after us calling, "Boys! Oh, boys!"

We went back. She had something in her hand, which she held out to me. Her eyes had that mischievous look again.

"I was thinking you could use this," she said.

I looked down at the bottle, which was made of fancy cut glass and had a gold cap shaped like a swan. The label said *Floral Fantasy*.

"It's perfume," Aunt Hilda said. "I suddenly remembered a trick we played on my brother. Oh, he was so mad at us!" She giggled, remembering. "What made me think of it is, he was a football player. J.R. and Morrie are on the school team, aren't they?"

Augie nodded.

"I thought I saw their pictures in the paper," Aunt Hilda said.

I looked at the perfume bottle again, stumped. I looked at Augie, who shrugged.

"Um, what are we supposed to do with it?" I asked.

"Oh, I'm sure you'll think of something," she said innocently, and turned to go.

Augie and I stood there, speechless.

"I want a full report afterward, you hear?" she said with a laugh.

"Yes, ma'am," I said.

Augie and I made two trips out to the woods with all the supplies we'd gathered so far, and put them in the fort. Then we took a couple of Unk's buckets and collected black walnuts. Augie told me that when they were ripe, they fell to the ground, but since they weren't, we had to shinny up into the trees to get them.

By then it was getting dark, so we hung out at the fort cooking hot dogs and talking over the details of the plan.

We still needed to get Herkimer.

And Herkimer's head.

There was one more big problem to solve. If Gerard was going to be there to watch the operation go down, we were going to have to figure out how to get his mother to let him come with us.

And she thought we were the rotten guys who had made Gerard cry.

13

The next morning, I was awake before Augie.
My mind was already racing like crazy. The second I
heard him yawning and stretching and moving around
in his sleeping bag, I said, "So today we go to Gerard's
house, right?"

"Right," said Augie.

"I was thinking you should do the talking."

Augie frowned. "Why me?"

"You know them better than I do."

"Nice try, Wyatt. Come on. We've gotta do it together. We're a team, right?"

I sighed. Neither of us was looking forward to seeing
Mrs. DeMuth after what had happened the last time.
"Okay," I said. "Deal."

"Let's get it over with," Augie said.

As soon as we'd eaten some bread and peanut butter,

we left the woods, got on our bikes, and headed for the DeMuths'.

Gerard and his mother were out in the yard when we pulled up. She was weeding, and Gerard was staring down at the concrete path that led from the street to their front door. Something really interesting had his attention, and he didn't even look up as we parked our bikes. Mrs. DeMuth did look up, and was glaring at us in a definitely unfriendly way as we walked closer.

Soon we could see that Gerard had two worms lined up next to each other, and was watching them carefully like he was waiting for them to do something.

Augie and I both said a cautious hello. Gerard saw us then, and his face broke into a smile. "Hi, Augie. Hi, Wyatt." He pointed to the worms. "It's a race."

"Cool," I said. "Who's winning?"

Gerard peered at the worms. "Nobody."

"You got lazy worms," said Augie. "That's the problem."

Gerard seemed to find this hilarious. "Lazy worms!" he repeated, laughing like crazy. "I got lazy worms! That's the problem! Mom, that's the problem! Lazy worms!"

Mrs. DeMuth smiled at him. It was as if she just

couldn't be mad when Gerard was happy. I felt the same way. I didn't know if it was the idea of lazy worms, or Gerard's laugh, or both, but Augie and I were cracking up, too.

When we'd settled down, Mrs. DeMuth looked at us with her eyebrows raised in a question, and it was obvious she was wondering what we were doing there. Augie, the rat, was playing dumb, so I finally spoke up.

"Um, Mrs. DeMuth, remember the last time we were here?"

"Yes," she said. Her voice sounded flat and cool.

Boy, that was a dumb way to start. As if she would forget how we made her son cry.

I plunged on. "Well, it was a misunderstanding. Really it was some other kids who were mean to Gerard. He was telling us what they did to him, and that's why he was crying."

Mrs. DeMuth still looked suspicious, but she was listening. "Are you referring to J.R. and Morrie?" she asked.

I nodded eagerly, and so did Augie.

"Those two have been bothering Gerard for years," she said with a mix of anger and sadness.

"It's not just Gerard," said Augie. "They bother us all the time, too."

Gerard was kneeling beside his worms, watching them intently. I couldn't tell if he was listening or not.

"So, anyway, we felt really bad because you thought we were being mean to Gerard—"

Still looking down at his worms, Gerard said, "Augie and Wyatt are not mean to Gerard."

Mrs. DeMuth smiled at him, then gave a little shrug and smiled at us. "Well, I'm very glad to hear that. Thank you, boys, for stopping over."

I guess she figured we were finished, because she turned back to her gardening.

"Well, see," I said, "we came over because we were wondering if Gerard could maybe—if he wants to, that is—if he could sleep out at our fort this weekend."

Mrs. DeMuth's mouth dropped open with surprise, but Gerard didn't waste any time.

"Yes! Yes! Gerard *does* want to sleep at the fort!" he said, nodding his head up and down and up and down really fast. "This weekend. *Yes*."

Mrs. DeMuth looked back and forth between her son and Augie and me. She seemed torn, like she wanted to believe what she was hearing, but wasn't sure she should. "Do you mean this? This isn't some kind of joke?"

"No, ma'am," said Augie. "Honest."

"No joke," I added.

"Gerard wants to, Mom. No joke!"

"Oh, lovey," she murmured. To Augie and me she said, "It would mean so much to him." She lowered her voice and continued, "You'll take care of him?" Her voice trailed off, then she finished, "You understand what I'm saying, don't you?"

I did understand, and I guess Augie did, too, because we both nodded our heads off, almost as fast as Gerard had been doing.

After that, Mrs. DeMuth had a lot more questions. But finally we got it all settled. She would bring Gerard to Al's at three on Friday, with his sleeping bag and his stuff. I promised I'd take my cell phone and we'd call to let her know everything was going okay, or if he wanted to come home for some reason. Since we didn't know exactly when Operation Doom would go down, we just said we'd call when it was time for her to pick him up.

"Okay, Gerard," I said when we were ready to leave. "See you Friday!"

"Okay! See you Friday!" Gerard repeated. "See you Friday!" he kept calling as we got on our bikes. "See you Friday!" Then, "Lazy worms!"

We rode away to the sound of Gerard's laughter.

14

Since it was Wednesday, Augie and I both had to go home for dinner and to spend the night. I was worried about leaving the fort unguarded, but Augie swore (not in the bad way) that J.R. and Morrie wouldn't show up during the week.

We decided to go home early and get started on our chores. We hoped Dad and Gram would be so impressed by this proof of our dedication that they'd have no hesitation about letting us stay at the fort over the weekend.

Still, I couldn't help worrying that all our plans would be for nothing. "What if they say no?" I fretted.

"They won't," said Augie. "We gotta think positive, Wyatt. That's what Gram always says anyhow."

As it turned out, Augie was right. When Dad got home at five, I had already taken the sheets off my bed and bagged them up with my dirty clothes, mowed the grass, and taken out the garbage. The garbage was part of our plan, and I was happy to note that it was good and ripe.

Dad brought home some chicken, so I lit the grill and helped him make salad and garlic bread. While we ate, he asked me what Augie and I had been up to, and I told him about inviting Gerard to sleep out at the fort. Dad's pretty cool, but I didn't see any reason to bring up Operation Doom.

"You're talking about—what?—Friday night?" he asked.

"Maybe Saturday, too," I said carefully. "If Gerard wants to."

"Well, I think that's a really nice thing for you boys to do," said Dad. "It's fine with me, as long as Mrs. DeMuth is comfortable with it. But— You know what? Take your phone. Just in case something unexpected happens."

"I already thought of that," I said eagerly. "I told Mrs. DeMuth we'd call her."

Dad nodded in approval.

And that was that. I could hardly believe it had been that easy. I called Augie.

"Gram said yes, too," he told me happily.

Everything was falling into place.

Dad and I played poker until he yawned and said, "I've got an early class to teach tomorrow, so we'd better hit the hay."

Like I said, Dad's pretty cool. Even when he says corny stuff like "hit the hay."

15

I was in the driveway waving goodbye to Dad when Augie showed up on his bike.

"Did you remember Herkimer?" I asked.

Augie pointed to a paper bag in the basket of his bike. "I put him in the bag in case we run into Unk."

I felt a pang of guilt about Unk's prize owl, lying decapitated all week in Bertha's trunk and now stuffed into a paper bag. "You got his head, too?" I asked.

"Well, duh," said Augie.

"You figure we'll fix him and sneak him back into the attic, right?" I said. "After the mission, I mean."

"Yeah," said Augie. "A little superglue and he'll be good as new."

"Okay," I said. "Well, I guess next is—the garbage."

We went to the end of the driveway and I took the lid

off the big plastic trash can I had taken out the night before.

I gestured to the can and then to Augie. "Ladies first."

Augie frowned. "Man, that *reeks*. Even through the bags!"

"The rottener the better, right?"

"I guess." Wrinkling his nose, Augie looked inside. Then he reached in and took one bag and I took another.

"So that's it," I said.

"Let's go."

Unk and Al weren't around yet, and we headed straight to the fort.

"Where do we start?" asked Augie.

"The first thing is to figure out where they're going to walk to get here," I said. "Which is kind of a no-brainer. They'll take the easiest, shortest route, just like we did when we first came in. They'll cross the field behind Al's and go through that opening in the trees at the edge of the woods, right?"

"Only logical," Augie agreed.

"Exactly. We know that last time they went from there toward the stream—"

"—because we know where they crossed and found the squirrel guts!" Augie finished. "And, besides, it's the easiest way. We did the same thing. So do the deer and other animals."

"Then, from the stream, it's sort of a straight uphill line to here," I said, pointing.

Augie nodded. "Let's go."

We got to work. I'd never realized before that playing chess and being good at math would come in handy in real life. But it turns out, knowing about angles and how to figure out distances and stuff can be very useful.

From chess I'd learned that you have to plan more than one move ahead of your opponent, and try to figure out what he might do before he does it. Add to that the fact that Augie knew everything in the world about the woods and hunting and all, and J.R. and Morrie didn't stand a chance!

We took a quick break for lunch, having cold dogs instead of hot dogs, which Augie said he liked better. While we were eating, we decided that planning Operation Doom was pretty much the most fun we'd ever had, and our victims hadn't even shown up yet.

"We can't help it if we're diabolical masterminds!" I declared.

"Genuine evil geniuses!" agreed Augie.

When we'd finished, we built a fire and sat around talking and laughing, imagining the way the operation would go down. I could hardly sleep, thinking about it. Augie fell right to sleep and was even snoring like some old geezer in a cartoon. I kept poking him. He'd stop for a second, make some weird noises, and then start up again. He was so sound asleep it made me think of the old trick where you put a sleeping person's hand in warm water, which for some reason—don't ask me why, but it's a scientific fact—causes him to go pee. But I didn't really want to do it to Augie. J.R. and Morrie, sure, in a heartbeat, if the opportunity came up. But not Augie.

Anyway, I noticed something as I was lying there. When you're sleeping out in a fort—only you're wide-awake, not sleeping—you hear a lot of strange noises. Besides the ones your snoring friend is making, I mean. These noises all sounded like they were made by something big. Something sneaky. Something sinister.

That night, every rustle of a leaf, every crack of a twig, every grunt and squeak meant that we'd figured it wrong and J.R. and Morrie were right outside the fort's walls, ready to pounce. It just didn't seem fair that I was the only one on high alert. I needed backup.

"Augie!" I whispered, jabbing him in the side.

"Zzzzz-snrkx-zzzz."

"Augie!" Another jab.

"Mmmm-waa-glrg-zzzzzzzzz."

"Augie!" Major jab.

"Wa-aa-mmm-zzzzz."

"Fine," I muttered. "You go right ahead and sleep. I'll just lie here awake so I can save your sorry butt when disaster strikes. No problem."

The next thing I knew, a bug or something was crawling across my face. I tried to ignore it and go back to sleep, but it wouldn't go away. Finally, I swatted at it and opened my eyes, only to see Augie's grinning mug five inches from mine. It was morning.

"Rise and shine, dude," he said, dangling the Slim Jim wrapper he'd been using to tickle my cheek. "We've got stuff to do!"

I groaned. "I can't believe you're waking me now after keeping me up all night with your snoring."

Through my half-closed eyes I saw Augie's look of dismay. "I do not snore!" he said.

"I got news for you, Augie."

"Whatever you heard, it wasn't me."

"Oh, so there was a dying warthog over there in your sleeping bag with you?"

"Don't you think I'd know it if I was snoring?"

"Actually," I said, trying to be reasonable, "no. Because *you were asleep.*"

"I know stuff, even when I'm asleep," Augie said.

"Look, I'm just telling you: you were snoring."

"I bet you were asleep and you were dreaming about me snoring."

"Augie, I wasn't asleep. That's the point. I was awake. *You* were asleep. And snoring. As Al would say, 'end of story.' What is the big deal?"

"I don't want to be a snorer," Augie said in a low voice.

"Why not?" I asked. I had been feeling exasperated, but now I was mystified. And curious.

"I just don't."

"No reason?"

"I don't like thinking I did something and I didn't even know I was doing it."

I thought about that.

"It creeps me out," Augie went on. "Like my body was taken over by an alien or something."

"Oh," I said. "Yeah, I kinda see what you mean."

Augie brightened up. "So I wasn't snoring after all?"

I decided to forget the whole thing right then and there. Augie was my right-hand man. We had a mission ahead. I didn't want him to be distracted. "No," I said. "You weren't. I must have dreamed the whole thing."

Augie nodded. "I thought so."

Geez. I was glad that was settled. It was time to get down to business.

16

"**There's something I thought of during the** night," I told Augie. "What do you say we get that big sign that used to be on the old ice cream stand, the one that was torn down and got junked at Al's?"

"The Pink Palace sign? What would we do with *that*?"

"Put it up here at the fort."

Augie's eyes narrowed as he thought about it. "J.R. and Morrie made a lot of fun of us when they saw the pink boards we were using."

"Exactly. But now we've got this awesome fort. I bet they wish it was theirs. So instead of being all embarrassed about it being pink, we make it, like, a—"

"A badge of honor!" Augie said.

I knew Augie would get it.

"Al already said we could have the sign, remember?" Augie went on.

"Yeah! I was thinking it would look really cool"—I crawled out the front of the fort and Augie followed—"if we attached it right *there*," I finished, pointing to the main support next to the door.

"Totally," said Augie.

We got dressed real fast and went through the woods down to Al's. The yard wasn't open yet, but the wood and the sign from the old ice cream stand had been dropped off after hours and were still lying in the driveway.

The sign was bigger than I remembered, about ten feet tall and six feet wide, with the words *The Pink Palace* outlined in metal, with empty sockets where lightbulbs used to be. We each grabbed one end and lifted it. Not too bad: it was more awkward than heavy.

Stopping to rest every couple of minutes, we made it to the fort. For the time being, until we figured out how to attach it more permanently, we leaned it against the side, where anyone coming the usual way would see it.

"Good, huh?" I asked.

Augie nodded solemnly. "Gram would like it," he said. "She likes finding uses for old stuff."

We goofed around for a while and had some breakfast. After that, we checked and rechecked all our preparations. We were as ready as we were ever going to be.

Then we played some poker. I had a run of really lousy cards, and my mind wandered to meeting up with Gerard that afternoon. I started getting nervous.

All of a sudden I wasn't sure having him with us was such a great idea. After what J.R. and Morrie had done to him, I had really wanted him to be there when we got them back. He deserved to be there. But still . . .

His mom had said Gerard just wanted to be like other kids. But he wasn't. Not exactly.

"Augie," I said, "what if Gerard starts to act . . . I don't know . . . *weird*?"

"What do you mean?"

"I don't know. I mean, what if he freaks out because he's scared of the dark or loses his rabbit's foot or something? I bet he's never spent the night away from home in a strange place. He's not used to going places and hanging out with his friends. Because—"

"He doesn't have any friends," Augie finished.

"Yeah," I said.

We were quiet for a minute.

I felt bad about Gerard not having friends. I would

never torture him and tease him, like J.R. and Morrie, or call him rotten names. But did I want to be his friend? I had a sudden fear, not of *him*, exactly, but of being responsible for him, even for a night. I couldn't explain it to myself and I sure wasn't explaining it very well to Augie.

"Well," said Augie after a while, "remember that night he was in your driveway? He was by himself and he wasn't scared of the dark then."

"Yeah, that's true."

"He's been out here to the fort before. And he wants to come back." He laughed. "He wants to come back really bad!"

I remembered Gerard's grin as he nodded his head yes. "Also true."

Augie shrugged. "So I think it'll be okay. If it's not, we call his mom."

"Hey," I said, suddenly remembering something. "We never made up a song for him."

"Maybe he forgot all about it," Augie said hopefully.

"Maybe," I said. "But I doubt it. Once Gerard gets something in his head, he seems to stick with it."

"Well, there's no time now," said Augie. "We gotta go."

When we got to the junkyard, we shot the breeze with Al and Unk for a while until Mrs. DeMuth pulled up. When Gerard got out of the car, smiling hugely, holding his squirrel tail in one hand and his rabbit's foot in the other, Al and Unk pretended to concentrate on their checkerboard, but I could tell they were busting to see and hear everything that was going on.

Mrs. DeMuth got out of the car, too, and we helped her unpack a sleeping bag, a backpack, and a giant cooler. By then Al and Unk weren't even pretending not to stare.

Gerard was talking a mile a minute, while his mom was asking us all the same questions she'd asked before. She looked really worried and uncertain. Suddenly she put her hand to her mouth and said, "Oh, dear. Maybe this isn't such a good idea after all."

I couldn't blame her. I'd had the same feeling, and I wasn't Gerard's mom. I mean, she sort of knew Augie, but she didn't know me much. And Gerard was her only kid. He'd been made fun of a lot. He'd never done anything like this before.

But Gerard was ready. "Let's *go*! Can we go now, please? To the fort? I'm all set, right, Mom? I got everything I need, don't I, Mom?"

To us, he said, "Can we go now? I got everything I need. I'm all set!"

Augie and I looked at Mrs. DeMuth. Her mouth quivered a little bit, but then she gave Gerard a big bright smile.

"You are all set, lovey," she agreed. To Augie and me, she said, "You'll call?"

We nodded.

She gave us a long gaze followed by a nod which said without words, *I'm counting on you two.*

Then she got in the car and drove away.

I handed Gerard his backpack. He put it on and picked up his sleeping bag. Augie and I looked at the cooler. It was one of those enormous rectangular ones, with handles on the sides.

"What's in that thing?" I asked.

"Food. And drinks. Growing boys need food and drinks," said Gerard. "That's what Mom said."

I opened the lid. "Wow." The cooler was packed. I saw wrapped packages of sandwiches and fried chicken, bottles of juice and chocolate milk, and there was a lot more stuff underneath that I couldn't see.

My mouth watered, looking at the fried chicken.

Roughing it was great, but there was something to be said for Gerard's mom's approach to camping.

As Augie and I examined the monster cooler, trying to figure out how to carry it, Al and Unk came strolling over. They both were carrying things, but I couldn't tell what.

"Tonight's the night?" Unk asked.

"We think so."

"You boys be careful now," he said. He looked worried.

"We will."

Al jerked his head ever so slightly in Gerard's direction and asked, "You sure you know what you're doing?"

Augie and I looked at each other. "Yeah, I guess," Augie said finally.

"Keep an eye on the matches," Al warned in a low voice.

If Al thought Gerard wouldn't hear him, he was wrong.

Gerard's eyes grew big. "Gerard does not like matches!"

"Glad to hear it," said Al.

"Here," said Unk, holding out a foil-wrapped package.

"Hilda made snickerdoodles and brownies. She said to wish you luck."

Augie took the package. "Wow. Tell her thanks."

Then Al held up something else.

"What is it?" I asked.

He brought it to his mouth and said, *"Ain't you never seen a bullhorn before?"*

We all jumped at the sudden blare of noise. Then Gerard started laughing like crazy. I guess he thought *bullhorn* was a pretty funny word, because he kept saying it over and over.

"It's been lyin' around my office for years," Al said. "You can have it if ya want. I even put in new batteries. It might come in handy." He shrugged. "It's loud, anyhow."

I took the bullhorn, pressed the button, and hollered into it, *"It sure is, Al!"*

Wow. It really was. I'd just about blasted my own eardrums out. It wasn't only loud. It distorted my voice so it sounded sort of tinny and alien-like, which was very cool.

"Smart guy," Al said, sticking his finger in his ear. He smirked and said, "Maybe I won't give ya this second thing I got here." He held his other hand behind his back.

"Aw, come on, Al," said Augie. "Let's see it."

"Yeah, come on, Al," I said. "What is it?"

Al teased us for a while, keeping his hand behind his back and looking from Unk to us and back again while we begged. "What do you think?" he asked Unk.

"Aw, give it to 'em," said Unk. "It's no use to us old geezers."

"Speak for yourself," said Al. But he brought his hand out from behind his back, and there was a calendar with a smiling girl on the front holding up a blue bottle of STP motor oil.

"It's from 1997," Al said. "But some things never grow old, right, boys?"

"Right!" Augie and I said together. Augie reached right out to take the calendar before Al could decide he wanted to reexamine the STP bottles of yesteryear after all.

"Thanks a lot, Al," we said.

"Can we *go* now?" Gerard asked impatiently.

"Yeah, we can go now," I told him, laughing. He was big, but he sure sounded like a little kid sometimes.

"You fellas watch yourselves," said Unk.

"I hope you scare the diapers off those two *stronzos*!" said Al.

"Those two *whats*?" I asked. I knew who he was talking about, but I liked the sound of the word and I wanted to know what it meant.

"*Stronzos*," Al repeated disgustedly. "*Cretinos. Idiotas. Testa mutos.*"

"Jerks," explained Unk. "Idiots." He rapped his knuckles on his head. "Dumbheads."

If you ask me, Italian has it all over English when it comes to insulting people.

"We will!" I said.

Augie and I each grabbed a side handle on the cooler and hobbled along with it, stopping to rest about every ten steps.

When we got close to the fort, Gerard ran ahead. By the time Augie and I got there, panting and sweating, he was already unrolling his sleeping bag. He carefully laid out the squirrel tail and the rabbit's foot on top of the bag, along with a plastic baggie of gummy worms. He sat, looking contented.

All I could think about was fried chicken. "I'm starving!" I said.

"Me, too," said Augie, opening the lid of the cooler. He pulled out a pile of sandwiches, the package of chicken, and three bottles of chocolate milk, and passed them around.

My mouth stuffed with chicken, I said to Gerard, "Man, this is the best fried chicken I ever had in my whole life."

"Totally," agreed Augie. "Even better than Gram's, but don't tell her I said that."

Gerard looked pleased and said, "Man, this is the best fried chicken Gerard ever had in his whole life, too!"

While we were stuffing our faces, we told Gerard we planned on getting back at J.R. and Morrie that night. At the mention of their names, his face got all squinched and scared looking.

"*Stronzos,*" he muttered.

I laughed, surprised. Gerard didn't miss much. "Yeah, well, we're gonna show those *stronzos* they can't mess with us—or with you—anymore."

His face brightened up a little, and when Augie and I told him about some of the things we had in store, he got a huge kick out of them. He kept on repeating everything we said, laughing his loud, sort of goofy laugh.

"Hey, listen," I said. "It must be close to five o'clock.

You said football practice lets out at four on Fridays, right, Augie?"

Augie nodded. "I was thinking they'll probably eat dinner first, but they could surprise us. They could be here any second."

"We want them to know we're here, so we should build a fire like we usually do," I said.

I stood up and started to gather some small sticks for kindling.

Augie said, "What's the matter, Gerard?"

I looked over, and Gerard's face had made one of its amazing transformations. A minute before, he'd been happy and laughing. Now his face was white, his chin was trembling, and his eyes were fluttering like they were going to start rolling back out of sight again.

Uh-oh.

It was just what I'd been afraid of. Gerard was freaking out.

17

"Gerard!" I hollered, not trying to scare him but hoping to snap him out of it before he had one of his little fits, or whatever they were. "What's wrong? Tell us!"

"G-Gerard d-does *not* like fires," he said.

I looked at Augie, like, *What the heck? This is the kid everybody says is a firebug?*

"Okay." I took a deep breath and plunged ahead. I *had* to ask. "But, well, you know what? Some people say you *do* like fires. They think you burned down some old shed at Al's place. Is that true?"

Gerard started crying. Oh, no. The situation was getting worse. I felt bad about making him cry, but geez. I looked to Augie for help.

"Um," he said to Gerard, "so you *don't* like fires?"

"*No!*" Gerard bellowed between sobs. "*Gerard does not burn fires! Gerard does not like fires!*"

It hit me that he wasn't crying like he was sad, though. More like he was angry. Or frustrated.

Like you might cry, I thought, *if you got blamed for something you didn't do.*

I turned to Augie, bewildered. "Why does everybody think he did it, then?"

"I don't know," he said. "Al said there was no proof who did it. Gram never believed it was Gerard. I guess I don't, either."

Looking at Gerard now, neither did I.

"Gerard," I said, trying to sound calm. "Remember you told us you didn't light the matches here at the fort?"

Gerard snuffled and nodded.

"And we believed you, right?"

He nodded again.

"It was J.R. and Morrie who lit the matches here, right?" Augie asked.

Gerard nodded again.

My heart was beating really hard as I asked, "Did they burn down the shed, too?"

"Yes!" said Gerard. "But they said it was Gerard. They said they saw Gerard do it. *But Gerard saw them. Gerard saw them!*"

"How come you never told anybody?" Augie asked.

Gerard looked scared. "They said they would do something bad to Gerard. They said they would hurt Gerard."

Augie shook his head. "Those jerks," he said softly.

"*Stronzos,*" I said.

Augie and I were quiet for a while, thinking. Gerard snuffled a little, then stopped crying.

"Listen, Gerard," I said, "we believe you. But now we have to pull off Operation Doom more than ever. You've got to show them you're not afraid of them."

Gerard looked uncertainly from me to Augie and back.

"So stage one of the operation is we need a fire. Okay if we make one?" Augie asked. "Just a little one?"

"We want J.R. and Morrie to know we're here, because then they'll be sure to come up here to try to torture us," I explained. "And that's exactly what we want them to do."

"They don't even know you're here," said Augie. "You're part of the surprise."

"Gerard is part of the surprise!" Gerard repeated.

I was relieved and glad to see that he was grinning happily again, like nothing had ever happened.

While Augie and I started making a fire, Gerard got his squirrel tail and rabbit's foot and held them, humming a little tune. He didn't sing the words, but I recognized the crummy "song" J.R. and Morrie had made up.

Hearing it made me mad all over again. Augie and I had promised Gerard we'd make up something better, but we'd been concentrating on other stuff.

The tune played in my head as I walked farther into the woods to get some bigger branches. Some words came to me. I mumbled them along with the tune. Then I hurried back, threw the branches in a pile, and got my notepad and pencil from the fort.

Augie looked at me curiously and Gerard asked, "Whatcha doin', Wyatt?"

"Hold on a sec," I said. "Let me think." I scribbled for a while, crossed some stuff out, scribbled some more.

"Okay," I said after a while. "Gerard, do you remember that stupid song J.R. and Morrie made up for you?"

Gerard looked up from the squirrel tail he was petting and said cautiously, "Gerard is not supposed to sing it anymore. It's a bad song."

"It is," I said. "And remember Augie and I said we'd make up a new one? A better one?"

164

Augie looked nervous.

Gerard nodded.

"Did you come up with something?" Augie asked hopefully.

"Maybe," I said. "What do you think of this?" To the same tune Gerard had been humming a minute before, I sort of half sang and half spoke the song I'd been working on.

When I finished, Augie was looking at me with his mouth hanging open. "Holy cow, Wyatt! I can't believe you just made that up!" he said. "Say it again."

I did.

"I am Gerard!" Gerard shouted when I'd finished.

"Darn right you are!" I said.

Gerard kept saying the words over and over while Augie and I finished making the fire. Gerard got a little worried when we first lit it, but after that he was fine, even though he didn't sit too close. We sat around eating the brownies and snickerdoodles from Aunt Hilda and examining the new calendar from Al—all the while remaining on high alert for any sounds of J.R. and Morrie approaching.

Al was right. Some things never do change. Not the STP annual calendar, anyway. It was the same, only with different ladies and different cars and trucks. It's a winning formula, and I can see why STP sticks with it.

We got up a few times to gather more wood. We called Gerard's mom to tell her we were fine. We listened. But the woods were quiet and peaceful, with not even a little wind to rustle the leaves. Soon, Gerard's head was nodding and Augie and I had to keep punching each other on the arm to stay awake.

I looked at my watch. It was almost ten thirty.

"What do you think?" I whispered to Augie. "Are they gonna come?"

"Doesn't look like it," Augie whispered back.

"Bummer. I want it to happen tonight."

"Me, too. You want to take turns keeping watch, just in case?"

"Good idea."

"Okay." Augie smiled sleepily. "You first."

"Thanks a bunch."

Augie and Gerard wriggled into their sleeping bags. I could tell by their breathing that they were asleep almost right away.

So there I was, the lone sentry, protecting the fort from enemy intruders.

18

Being on guard was actually pretty cool. I looked to see that Augie's backpack and mine were close at hand, and checked again to make sure everything we needed was in them. Then I stared into the darkness, every muscle and nerve on edge.

After a while, it's possible that my eyes closed for a few seconds.

Because suddenly my head snapped up and I sat bolt upright. Voices! Then I saw flashlight beams. They were headed across the field behind Al's toward the entrance spot to the woods.

I leaned into the doorway of the fort and whispered, "Wake up! They're coming!"

Augie was awake in a second. He grinned in the firelight.

Gerard took a little longer to stir, but soon he was sitting up, eyes wide with excitement.

We all listened. I was straining my ears so hard I thought my head would explode.

There was nothing for a while, except the occasional crack of a twig and the sweeping of the flashlight beams as J.R. and Morrie moved slowly through the woods.

Then there was a loud thud and an "Oooof!" followed by "Stupid branches!"

Then some pretty bad words rang through the night.

"Did you hear that?" I said. "One of them hit the first trip wire!"

Al's two-word tip had been "Trip wires." On the library's computer, we'd found a ton of information about them. It turns out they're pretty simple to set up. Like, you can set one up in your victim's path, using invisible fishing line. You can tie one end to something that will fall on your victim, or jump up or swing down to scare him when he trips the wire by walking into it.

Or you can use something stronger for your wire and actually trip the person.

In wars, like the one in Vietnam, soldiers set them so that giant rocks would fall on the enemy, or sharp spikes would impale them, or a giant blade would swing down and chop off their heads. Or the wire might set off a gun or a grenade or something.

When we'd gotten to that part, Augie had whispered, "Geez, Wyatt. I mean, I know this is war. And I hate those guys. But I don't want to chop off their heads or anything like that."

"Yeah," I'd said. "Me neither."

That was when we'd agreed on our no damage, no death, no dismemberment policy.

So the first trip wire we'd set was a simple one, designed to do exactly that—trip the first person who stepped into it.

"That voice sounded like J.R. to me," I whispered.

"Couldn't happen to a nicer guy," Augie replied.

This made Gerard laugh like crazy. Seeing him so happy was great, but I was afraid J.R. and Morrie might hear him, so I put my fingers to my lips to show him we needed to try to stay quiet.

We could hear the rise and fall of J.R.'s and Morrie's voices, growing closer.

Then one of them, Morrie, I think, called out, "You girls having fun in your pink fort?"

"Quick, hide your dollies," yelled J.R. "We're coming to pay a little visit."

"No!" I called, making myself sound real scared. "Don't come up here!"

"Yeah, get outta here," hollered Augie. "This is *our* fort."

"Hang on to your flashlight," I whispered to Gerard, "but don't turn it on."

We all stepped out into the darkness and crept quietly in the direction we thought they'd be coming from, but not too far yet.

To Augie I said, "Ready?"

"Oh, yeah!" he replied.

After a couple of seconds, we heard a shower of thumps followed by "Ouch!"

"Ow!"

"Whoa!"

"What the—?"

"What's going on?"

Followed by more thumps and some curses.

This meant that the wire to the bucket of black walnuts had been tripped. We'd gathered at least a hundred of them. They were round—somewhere between the size of a golf ball and a lacrosse ball—and really hard. The entire bucketful had just fallen on J.R.'s and Morrie's heads. Which probably didn't feel so hot. Then, as they tried to run away, they kept stepping on rolling walnuts and falling down.

To Augie I said, "Ready? Fire!"

One by one, we each took the balloons we had blown up and stashed in our backpacks and popped them—Augie with his pocketknife and me with a knife from our kitchen. I handed a couple to Gerard and said, "Stomp on them!"

It was kind of amazing how loud the *pops* sounded, carrying through the quiet night woods.

We heard J.R.'s and Morrie's cries—

"What was that?"

"Were those *shots*?"

"Is somebody *shooting*?"

There were grunts and more thumps as they stepped on the rolling walnuts in their hurry to get away, fell, tried to get up, and fell again.

In my mind, I could see it as plain as day, in spite of the darkness. It was beautiful.

"Valerio," J.R. shouted, "you are such dead meat."

"You, too, Jones," snarled Morrie.

I wasn't worried. Because next, if all went according to plan, they would trip another wire, which was attached to another bucket—

"Wait for it . . ." I whispered.

"*Ewwwww—gross!*"

"Disgusting!"

"*Yes!*" said Augie. "They tipped the garbage bucket!"

Howls of anger filled the night, along with some words I was sorry Gerard was hearing. He didn't seem to be bothered, though. In fact, he was yukking it up, with his hands over his mouth to stifle the sound.

We had calculated that by this point, J.R. and Morrie would be disoriented and would no longer be moving in a direct route toward the fort. So we didn't know which wire they might hit next: the one that would tip over a half gallon of Gram's honey, or the one with Aunt Hilda's perfume mixed with soapy water.

The timing on the honey bucket had been extra tricky. We'd figured the thick honey would ooze more slowly from the bucket than the perfumed water would, so it had to be situated in a tree farther away from where J.R. or Morrie actually tripped the wire, in order to be sure it would plop on their heads. Lots of angles and several hooks and eyes were involved.

We listened carefully, watching J.R.'s and Morrie's flashlight beams zigging and zagging through the trees. We had made our calculations about the path J.R. and

Morrie would take, based on the idea that people and animals always take the easiest path. If we were real lucky—and they were very unlucky—they would come the same way. J.R. would tip one bucket and Morrie the other.

"Looks like they both may be dead on course!" Augie said, poking me in the ribs. And from the screams and threats we heard next, I knew he was right.

We had discussed the possibility that J.R. and Morrie would surrender at that point, turn around, and go home, drenched in either garbage or perfume, and dripping honey. If that happened, it would definitely count as a victory. But we really hoped they kept on coming.

"Don't come up here!" I called again.

"You wish!" Morrie roared.

"You two are going to be sorry you were ever born!" an enraged J.R. hollered.

Augie and I cracked up, and Gerard joined in with his excited, high-pitched laugh.

I checked the fire to make sure it was still burning brightly enough to act as a beacon to keep the enemy coming straight for the fort. It was.

"Come on," I said. "Let's go."

Trying not to make a sound, Augie, Gerard, and I

started to move toward J.R. and Morrie. We shuffled very slowly at first, in a line—Augie first, feeling his way, Gerard between us, and me last.

There were still a couple of simple trip wires J.R. and Morrie could run into, bonus traps we'd added just to aggravate and embarrass them even more. But the best trick of all was waiting, the one we were sure would send them running, crying like babies, never to return.

Augie led us on toward the place in the woods where the final trap was set. We tried to be careful and not make any noise. But we really didn't have to worry much about keeping quiet. J.R. and Morrie had managed to hit a few more of the wires, and their groans, shouts, and cusses echoed through the trees.

"We're here," Augie whispered.

"Gerard," I said, "kneel right here by this fallen tree. Keep your head down out of the beams of their lights. Stay here. Be super quiet, and don't move until I tell you, okay?"

Gerard nodded. He had a huge grin on his face and was wriggling all around, practically doing a little dance, he was so excited.

I grinned back at him, suddenly really glad he had come along.

When Gerard was all set, Augie and I took up our positions. I stood behind the trunk of a tall tree, Augie behind another about twenty yards away. We held our flashlights ready. My cell phone was ready, too, sticking out of the top of my shirt pocket where I could grab it in a hurry.

J.R. and Morrie were charging through the woods in our direction, crashing wildly through the underbrush in their rush to get to the fort—and us.

"You little wusses are in for a world of pain," J.R. shouted. From the anger in his voice I could tell this wasn't a game to him anymore, if it ever had been.

My heart was beating so hard, it felt like a flock of birds was flying around in my chest. I'll admit it: part of me wanted to turn and run. But I reminded myself what we had in store for them, and I stood my ground.

The enemy was coming right toward us, just as we had hoped. I said a silent prayer that Gerard would re-member to stay absolutely still and quiet.

J.R. and Morrie were so close by then we could hear them panting. Augie and I stayed behind our trees, out of reach of their flashlight beams, waiting, waiting, waiting for the perfect moment . . .

Then, as spookily as I could, I called, *"Hoo-hoo-hoo. Hoo-hoo!"*

J.R.'s and Morrie's footsteps came to a halt.

"What the heck was that?

"Hoo-hoo-hoo. Hoo-hoo."

Quickly, J.R. and Morrie pointed their flashlights around in all directions.

"Up there!"

"What *is* that?"

Both flashlight beams now shone directly up into the tree branches over Augie's head.

Now! I sent a silent message to Augie.

And as if he'd heard me, there was a sudden—

Whoooosh!

Herkimer's large feathered body came swooping down from the tree, right past J.R.'s and Morrie's faces.

A shrill shriek of terror filled the night.

We could see everything in the glow cast by the two flashlight beams, even though one had now fallen to the ground.

Then Herkimer came swinging back.

I didn't know if Augie was adjusting the fishing line we'd attached to Herkimer's body or if it just worked out that way, but when the owl swung back the third time, his claws tangled in J.R.'s hair.

J.R. screamed and batted the body away, only to have it swing back toward him again.

"Help! Get it off me!"

Aaah. Music to my ears.

J.R. was freaking out, swatting wildly at the owl's swinging body, yelling, *"Get off me!"*

I thought I heard a burst of laughter from Gerard, and I couldn't blame him. It didn't matter, what with all the other noise and confusion.

J.R. was crawling on the ground, desperate to get away from his attacker. Morrie was focusing his light on Herkimer, who was now swinging in smaller and smaller arcs. I saw some loose feathers drifting through the air.

Morrie stood still, looking scared and nervous as he watched Herkimer slowly swing to a stop. Then he walked closer and reached out tentatively, as if he was afraid whatever it was might move again. At that moment, it *did*, as Augie released his end of the fishing line and Herkimer's body fell to the ground at Morrie's feet. He stepped back with a cry of surprise, then bent down and picked it up.

"What *is* it?" croaked J.R.

"Some kind of bird," Morrie answered. Sounding uneasy, he added, "With no head."

Before he could notice the fishing line attached to Herkimer's body, I loosened the end of another line that led to a screw eye high up on the trunk of my tree, and slowly let out several feet. I could feel the answering pressure as Augie, from his position in the tree across from me, took up the slack.

J.R. and Morrie stood frozen in place, staring in mute terror, looking as if they couldn't believe what they were seeing—or didn't want to.

From high in my tree, an eerie apparition floated sideways and downward, right past J.R.'s and Morrie's faces. It was Herkimer's head, with his yellow glass eyes staring and his beak open as if he was about to attack. From behind his tufted ears billowed a scrap we had torn from Aunt Hilda's nightgown. It was so thin and gauzy it seemed to be there one minute and gone the next. The effect was even creepier than Augie and I had hoped.

I pulled on the line again, and the head glided back in my direction. Then it was Augie's turn. The head swayed gently and started back toward him. The rubber band that connected it to the fishing line caused it to bob in a weirdly convincing and lifelike way.

I reached for my phone, touched the camera icon, and called, "Say cheese!" My camera's flash lit up the darkness. Quickly, I checked the image. *Yes!* I had captured Morrie's eyes bulging in panic and J.R.'s mouth hanging slack with fear. But—even better—the picture showed:

Their ripped shirts and the stained and shredded knees of their pants.

The dirt and leaves and pine needles stuck in the honey that dripped from Morrie's face and hair and clothing.

The scraps of rotten lettuce, moldy cheese, and unrecognizable goo that decorated J.R.'s shoulders.

And the piece of greasy chicken skin dangling from his ear.

"Gotcha!" I said. "It's a lovely photo of you both!"

I only wished that phone technology had advanced so I could have captured the smells, too. The odors of Floral Fantasy (from Morrie's direction) and putrefied garbage (from J.R.'s) floated around them in a cloud so thick you could almost see it.

I also wished I could see Augie's face and Gerard's right at that minute. Operation Doom had gone off with military precision! Everything had worked like a charm! We had done it!

And we had the picture to prove it.

Now was the moment when J.R. and Morrie would flee in shame and terror, desperate to escape from their tormenters—which, this time, was *us*! Now they would run, wanting only to get out of these woods and never come back! Now they would make their mad dash to safety, and they would never bother Augie or me or Gerard again. Not as long as we had that photo.

I savored the moment, watching and waiting.

J.R. turned to Morrie. They exchanged a long look.

Ha! Just as we thought! They were agreeing: it was time to get the heck out of Dodge.

"Bye-bye, boys!" I called gleefully.

But—I couldn't believe it! Instead of leaving, they charged!

Morrie grabbed Augie. J.R. grabbed me.

And they began beating the snot out of us.

19

Things happened awfully fast after that. J.R. had knocked me down and was on top of me. His hands, sticky with garbage, were rummaging through my pockets.

"Gimme that phone," he grunted.

Now, you might imagine that at this point I'd be thinking of ways to save my skin. But that weird part of my brain that comes up with crazy stuff at the worst possible times was wondering how come I got stuck with J.R., who smelled even worse than he looked, while Augie got Morrie, who was drenched in Floral Fantasy. If I was going to die, I wondered, why couldn't my last vision be of Aunt Hilda? Why couldn't the sweet scent of her perfume fill my dying nostrils, instead of the stench of a Dumpster?

But then I heard gasping and struggling nearby, and Morrie's voice saying, "Prepare to die, Lame-o." And I knew Augie was having problems of his own.

"Gimme the phone," J.R. demanded again.

"No way," I said between clenched teeth, surprising myself with my bravery in the face of imminent death. That phone was our only hope of getting out of this, and I wasn't going to just hand it over.

While he tried to get at the pants pocket where I'd jammed the cell phone for safekeeping, I fought to get free of him. He smelled so bad, I had to concentrate on not breathing through my nose, for fear I'd throw up. Throwing up might have been a useful tactic, actually, but I never had to test it out.

Because suddenly a terrifying roar burst through the night.

I thought of Al, warning us that sometimes at night bloodcurdling screams came from the woods, sounding like somebody getting their heart ripped out by a wild animal while they were still alive. Is that what we were hearing?

I froze. J.R. froze in his position on top of me. The sounds of battle coming from Morrie and Augie went silent.

Then, breaking the utter stillness and quiet, a voice bellowed:

"*Be on your guard!*"

It *was* Gerard! On Al's bullhorn! No wonder his voice sounded so loud—and so weird and robot-like. He'd started reciting the words to the song I'd made up that afternoon. There was a long pause. Oh, no. Had he forgotten the rest?

Come on, Gerard, I urged him silently. *I heard you saying the words over and over. Keep going!*

"*'Cause I am Gerard!*"

Another pause. *Come on, Gerard!*

"*I know the liars
Who like to set fires.*"

From above me, I heard J.R. gasp.

"*I kept my mouth shut
Up until now, but—*"

Long pause.

J.R.'s breathing got faster.

"Be on your guard—
'Cause I AM GERARD!"

There was complete silence for a few seconds. Then I could feel the air go out of J.R., like he was a big stinky balloon deflating on top of me. I wriggled out from under him, and he stood up, kind of shakily.

Morrie let go of Augie and got up, very slowly and carefully, keeping a wary eye on Augie the whole time. I guess he wanted to make sure Augie wasn't going to retaliate by punching his lights out.

I have to admit, it *was* tempting. But Augie and I both stood by our no damage policy, which I would just like to point out shows a lot of self-control on our parts.

Morrie stood. He was panting. There was a confused look on his face, which matched J.R.'s dazed expression.

If I had drawn a thought bubble over Morrie's head right then, it would have said: *Uhhhh, what the heck just happened?*

One over J.R.'s head would have read: *Uhhhh, what do we do now?*

It was pretty funny, but I figured laughing might not be the best move, no matter how unthreatening J.R. and Morrie looked at that moment.

I glanced anxiously at Augie, who was on his feet by then. He didn't look too bad. His shirt was ripped and his cheek looked a little red, but there was no blood. He gave me a quick grin. No missing teeth. I felt better.

At that moment, Gerard's voice blared out, singing his song all over again, faster this time.

> *"Be on your guard,*
> *'Cause I am Gerard.*
> *I know the liars*
> *Who like to set fires.*
> *I kept my mouth shut*
> *Up until now, but—*
> *Be on your guard,*
> *'Cause I AM GERARD!"*

That last *Gerard!* was super loud. I couldn't help smiling. When Gerard got something in his head, he sure liked to stick with it, which could sometimes drive you nuts. But in this case, it was perfect. When he said the part about the fires, I watched the same expression appear on both J.R.'s and Morrie's faces. It was the look of a cornered rat.

Gerard's voice had sounded closer and closer. Now that the song was finished, he emerged suddenly from the darkness. He'd always been big. But right then he looked *enormous*, towering over us in that clearing in the woods. And, well, *scary*. He was holding his flashlight under his chin so that it cast ghoulish shadows across his big white face.

He looked unfamiliar.

He looked *fierce*.

"Gerard?" I said, before I could stop myself.

He smiled, but that only made him look even creepier.

I noted with interest that J.R. and Morrie were staring at him with something like horror.

I caught Augie's eye, then started talking, hoping he'd help out if I got stuck on what to say.

"So, gentlemen," I said. I sounded a lot more sure of myself than I actually was. I don't even think my voice was shaking, which it totally was, inside. "Here's the situation. Our friend Gerard told us the whole story about seeing you guys set fire to Al's shed. And about how you scared him into keeping quiet."

An idea crossed my mind right then, and I plunged ahead, making it up as I went along. "Then you two spread the rumor that Gerard was the one who did it, trying to make sure no one would believe him, even if he did talk."

J.R. and Morrie exchanged a furtive glance. Bingo! I had been right.

Augie flashed me a thumbs-up sign.

I was on a roll! "So here's what's going to happen. You're not ever going to mess with Gerard or us again. Because if you do, Gerard talks. And I guarantee, people will believe him."

Augie jumped in. "You know Coach's code of conduct. When he finds out about what you did, you'll be off the football team so fast you won't know what happened."

My turn to give him a thumbs-up.

"But first," he added, "the other guys on the team might be interested in seeing that picture Wyatt took tonight. How did it come out, Wyatt?"

"Oh, it's just *perfect*," I said, waving the phone in the air. To J.R. and Morrie I added, "Just take a look at each other if you want the general idea. Only your faces look like *this*." I opened my eyes and mouth in my best imitation of a victim in a horror movie.

Morrie made a sudden lunge at me, in an attempt to grab the phone. But Gerard, who had been standing by, shining his flashlight on J.R. and Morrie, roared through the bullhorn, *"Stop right there, stronzo!"*

Morrie did. He looked puzzled. "What'd he call me?"

"You don't want to know," I said.

J.R. had just about jumped out of his skin at Gerard's sudden shout. Now he stood, shaking, his eyes bugging out. So quietly we could barely hear him, he said, "I'm outta here. You coming, Morrie?"

Morrie took one long look around, like he was trying to think of something that would give him the final advantage. But he had nothing, and he must have known it.

Gerard, Augie, and I watched them disappear into the darkness. They went a lot more slowly than they had come, picking their way very carefully and flashing their lights ahead and up into every tree.

We did a three-way high five before busting into uncontrollable laughter. I don't know about Augie and Gerard, but I didn't realize how nervous and scared I'd been until it was over. I was relieved and kind of stunned that we had actually pulled it off, and all I could do was laugh. Gerard and Augie, too. Every time one of us thought we had it together, somebody else would say or do something to start us going again.

It was epic.

Eventually we went back to the fort, where we passed my phone back and forth to look again at the picture of J.R. and Morrie. Then we took some shots of us goofing around by The Pink Palace sign. Then we built up the fire and sat around eating and reliving every minute of Operation Doom.

Finally, we got quiet and sat staring happily into the dying embers of the fire.

Suddenly Gerard spoke. "This is the best night of Gerard's whole life."

"Mine, too," I said.

"Totally," said Augie.

20

We had a bunch of stuff to clean up in the
morning, but we didn't care. It was actually kind of
fun, because every empty bucket, every piece of fishing
line, and every popped balloon reminded us of our tri-
umph over the forces of evil.

It was fun, that is, until we came to Herkimer.

Or what was left of Herkimer.

"Aw, man," said Augie, picking up Herkimer's body
from the ground, which was strewn with feathers. He
held up the partially flattened owl. "Somebody stomped
on him."

One foot had snapped and was dangling limply from
Herkimer's leg. His wings were bent and broken looking. The feathers that remained were covered in dirt.

Augie stared with disbelief at the thing in his hand.

I unhooked the head from where it hung from the

wire, bobbing gently at the end of its rubber band. An eye was missing, and the beak was twisted to one side. It looked like the head of a grotesque bride with Aunt Hilda's nightgown trailing behind for a veil.

I didn't need to say it: a little superglue was *not* going to make Herkimer as good as new.

Not even close.

Gerard, looking sorrowful, took the body from Augie and patted it soothingly, the same way he did with his squirrel tail and rabbit's foot.

Augie was close to tears. "What am I going to tell Unk?" he moaned.

"We'll just have to tell him what happened," I said. "I'll go with you."

He nodded, but he didn't look any happier. I wasn't feeling too great about it myself.

We finished up, then stood around putting off the moment when we had to go see Unk.

"Let's just get it over with," I told Augie. "Better than sitting around here all day worrying about it anyway."

"Yeah," said Augie mournfully. "I know."

Gerard called his mother to say we were leaving. He began nodding his head enthusiastically, and I guessed she had asked him a question. He was nodding his answer, not thinking about how she couldn't see him over the phone. She must have asked again because then he said, "It was the best night of Gerard's whole life!"

Augie and I laughed. Whatever Unk was going to do to us on account of wrecking Herkimer, it had been worth it.

Nobody was around when we got to Al's. We waited for Mrs. DeMuth to come for Gerard, and told her how awesome her fried chicken was.

"I don't think J.R. and Morrie will be bothering Gerard anymore," I told her as we put the cooler and Gerard's stuff into the backseat of her car.

"If they *do*," added Augie, "you be sure to let us know."

"Be on your guard," Gerard shouted loudly, " 'cause I am Gerard!"

"You bet you are," Augie and I said together.

We waved goodbye and were ready to grab our bikes when Al appeared at the door to his office. His clothes were rumpled and his hair—or what he had left of it anyway—was sticking out all over the place, and he was rubbing his eyes, as if he'd just gotten up.

"Hey, Al," we called.

"What's going on?" Augie asked.

"Nothin' much," Al said as he tucked in his shirt-tails.

"You look like you just got out of bed," said Augie.

Al turned and gestured into the office. "Do you see a bed in there?"

"Well, what I meant was, you look like you were asleep."

"What are you, my boss, busting me for sleeping on the job?"

Augie looked confused. "So you *were* asleep," he said.

"Is there a law says I can't?"

Now Augie looked bewildered. "No. I was just— Never mind. Um . . . Unk's not here, is he?"

"You think I'm hiding him under the bed that isn't here either?" Al asked.

We were all quiet for a minute. Augie and I looked at each other. I knew he was thinking the same thing I was: What was Al so grouchy about?

Finally, Al broke the silence, asking casually, "Everything go okay last night?"

"Yeah," I said.

"Great," said Augie.

Al nodded. "Good. Now get outta here."

And suddenly I knew. Al *had* been asleep. He'd spent the night in his office so he'd be nearby in case anything went wrong. Maybe that was why he'd given us the bullhorn, so we could call for help. I was pretty sure the reason he was acting so grumpy was because he didn't want us to guess what he'd been up to.

I couldn't help smiling. The fact that it appeared Al had slept through the whole thing wasn't what mattered. What mattered was that he'd been there.

"Hey, Al," I said. "Guess what? We found out who burned down your shed, and it wasn't Gerard."

"No kiddin'?" he said. "Who?" Then he put it all together. "Those two *stronzos*?"

"Yep," Augie and I both said together. We told him the whole story.

"I shoulda known," muttered Al, shaking his head angrily. "Ya know what? Burning my shed—that's arson, by the way—that's crummy enough. But what really blisters my butt is the way they blamed it on that poor kid."

He thought for a moment. "Truth is, I was actually happy to get rid of that old thing. Them burning it saved me the trouble of knockin' it down and cartin' it away."

Then he laughed. "But ya think I'm gonna let *them* know that? Not on your great-grandma's girdle."

He smiled evilly. "They think they've gotten away with something? Well, guess what? Just 'cause your buddy Gerard is keeping his mouth shut doesn't mean *I* am." He pointed to his big barrel chest as he said this.

"I think later today I'll be having a little talk with those kids' parents about the very valuable building their sons destroyed on my property, and the work they're going to have to do for me to pay off the damage."

Al looked at Augie and me and nodded with satisfaction at his plan. "Ya mess with Al Juliano and ya find out what it means to mess with fire, am I right?"

"Absolutely," we agreed.

21

Then it was time to face the music. Glumly, Augie put his backpack, which held the battered parts of Herkimer, into the basket of his bike, and we rode to the Heindels' house.

Aunt Hilda came to the door, and we told her we needed to talk to Unk. She led us back to the bathroom, where he was busy painting, a brush in his hand and a roller sitting in a tray by the sink.

"Lemon Zest," he said gloomily, pointing the brush at the bright yellow walls. "With Summer Sunset trim."

I felt sorry for him. "It looks nice," I said.

"Yeah, nice," said Augie.

"So what's up?" Unk asked. "How did it go with J.R. and Morrie?"

"Oh, yes!" said Aunt Hilda, her eyes sparkling. "Did you teach those boys a lesson?"

Taking turns, we told them the whole story—well, not actually the whole story, not at first. We told them all the good parts: about the different booby traps, and about Gerard, and how he'd been blamed for the fire but didn't do it, and how he scared off J.R. and Morrie. Unk got a big kick out of hearing how well his paint buckets had worked, and Aunt Hilda loved hearing how Morrie got doused with her perfume. I showed them the picture on my phone.

Augie had so far avoided mentioning Herkimer, and I took my cue from him. I figured he would, once he'd worked up his courage.

Aunt Hilda said, "So did that nightie of mine come in handy?"

I waited to see what Augie would say.

"It worked great!" he answered, without thinking. Then, realizing it was time, he hung his head and his voice got low. "Well, actually . . . there's something I've got to tell you about that."

As Augie talked, I looked down at the floor, which was covered with a paint-spattered tarp. I know it was chicken of me, but they were going to be angry or, at the very least, disappointed in us, and I didn't want to see it on their faces until I had to.

When he'd finished, Augie opened his backpack and put the two parts of Herkimer's remains on the countertop next to the sink. The lone yellow glass eye seemed to be glaring right at me. The body, squashed and broken and patchy with missing feathers, looked like roadkill.

There was a long silence while Unk and Aunt Hilda took in the gruesome sight.

Finally, Unk made a funny croak in his throat. I think he was trying to say, "Herkimer." Then he swallowed hard. "I-I-" he stuttered, then said softly, "I don't know what to say."

"Well, I do!" declared Aunt Hilda. "I'm sorry, Heinie. I know you loved that nasty, disgusting old bird, but I've wanted it out of my attic for years."

Unk looked again at the two mangled parts of his beloved owl and sighed deeply. Then he handed Augie his paintbrush. He gave me the roller. "When you've finished here," he said, "I imagine Hilda can come up with another room that needs painting."

Augie and I watched as he left the room, his shoulders sagging.

"Gosh, Aunt Hilda," said Augie. "I feel really bad about this."

"Me, too," I said.

"Oh, don't you boys worry," said Aunt Hilda. "I'll bake him some snickerdoodles and he'll cheer up in no time." She smiled naughtily and whispered, "Meanwhile, I'm so grateful to you boys, I just don't know how to thank you!"

I didn't know about Augie, but I had an idea of how she could thank me. And, amazingly, it happened, just as I had imagined it would. Smiling, Aunt Hilda reached out, clasped me in her arms, and hugged me tightly to her in a warm, pillowy, floral-scented embrace that I'm sure I will remember for the rest of my life.

So that's it: the 100 percent true story about Augie and me and our fort and the best summer vacation I ever had.

I called Augie last night to see how everybody's doing, and he said good. He told me J.R. and Morrie have been real quiet. They haven't bothered him at all. Or Gerard either. I guess Al's been keeping them busy working at the junkyard.

Mostly we talked about what we'll do next summer. We've already come up with a plan. Somebody ditched an old boat at the junkyard when Al wasn't there. Al says it's a worthless old worm-box, but Augie's pretty sure we can fix it up.

FORT

Bonus Materials

GOFISH

QUESTIONS FOR THE AUTHOR

CYNTHIA DeFELICE

What did you want to be when you grew up?
Happy. That was it. No further ambitions.

When did you realize you wanted to be a writer?
Not until I was 36. Talk about late bloomers! I was working as a school librarian, which I loved, when I suddenly KNEW I wanted to try to write the kinds of books I loved sharing with my students.

Where did you get the idea for *Fort*?
My kids grew up in a small, safe, isolated neighborhood in the country. They and their friends had a fort called the Villa. We grown-ups didn't know exactly who built it, or when, or much of what went on there. It was a secret place for several generations of kids. We never found out the true story of how it burned down, although there are many legends that still circulate around here. When the characters Wyatt and Augie began taking shape in my head, it was fun to imagine the kind of fort they might build—on their own, and without much money or help from grown-ups—and what they would do there.

Did you build forts when you were a kid?
I had a couple forts. One was under the Ping-Pong table down in our dark and somewhat creepy basement. My favorite fort didn't require any construction. There was a circle of dense cedar trees in our yard. Once I was inside the circle, no one could see me. It was a terrific secret hangout, a place where I often pretended to be a pioneer girl. Ground-up acorn paste spread on oak leaves was a favorite "meal."

As a young person, who did you look up to most?
My dad, who was a good listener and very understanding.

What was your worst subject in school?
Math. Shudder. I still have math anxiety.

What was your best subject in school?
Surprise—English!

What was your first job?
Working in a bookstore in high school.

How did you celebrate publishing your first book?
Oh, I worked the celebrating to death! We celebrated the acceptance phone call. Then the contract. Then the advance check. The first galleys. The first review. Publication. And on and on. Champagne, ice cream, you name it!

Where do you write your books?
In my office, second floor of my house on Seneca Lake. I am deeply attached to my office and find it difficult to write anywhere else.

Which of your characters is most like you?
Allie Nichols from my Ghost Mysteries series—except that she is much braver, smarter, and cooler than I ever was!

When you finish a book, who reads it first?
My husband. He's a good critic. And I love getting the male point of view.

Are you a morning person or a night owl?
I'm a morning person for sure. I go to bed pathetically early.

What's your idea of the best meal ever?
Shrimp or fish pulled fresh from the ocean and cooked right then on the grill on the boat.

Which do you like better: cats or dogs?
No contest: dogs. I really enjoyed writing about Hoover, Mr. Henry's golden retriever, in the books about Allie Nichols.

What do you value most in your friends?
Humor, brains, and honesty.

Who is your favorite fictional character?
I first read *To Kill a Mockingbird* when I was in fifth grade, and Boo Radley still haunts me.

What are you most afraid of?
Giving a dumb answer to a question like this one.

What time of year do you like best?
Fall, because that's when we go on our summer vacation!

SQUARE FISH

What's your favorite TV show?
NFL football.

What's the best advice you have ever received about writing?
Plan on throwing out most of what you write.

What do you want readers to remember about your books?
The characters.

What would you do if you ever stopped writing?
I hope to work with horses or dogs, and volunteer to teach adults to read.

Where in the world do you feel most at home?
I crave being outdoors.

What do you wish you could do better?
I would love to be able to play a musical instrument well, and I'd love to be an accomplished horsewoman. These are both VERY distant goals. So distant that I think I'll need to wait for my next life.

When his army parents are deployed to the Middle East, twelve-year-old Erik goes to live with his grandparents, whom he barely knows, in a small town in North Dakota. But when he rescues a dog that his grandparents forbid him to keep, Erik runs away, taking the dog and a shotgun, certain they can make it on their own.

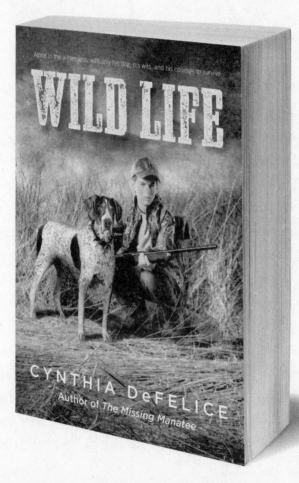

Alone in the wilderness, with only his dog, his wits, and his courage to survive

WILD LIFE

CYNTHIA DeFELICE
Author of *The Missing Manatee*

Keep reading for a sneak peek.

1

I passed!" Erik Carlson flew through the back door and into the dark kitchen hollering, "Mom! Dad! I passed!"

The screen door slammed shut behind him, rattling the cups in the dish drainer, causing the cat to leap from his perch on the windowsill and head for cover in the pantry closet.

"Oh, Crenshaw, don't be such a scaredy-cat," Erik called over his shoulder as he ran through the room.

He liked Crenny well enough when she decided to sit on his lap and allow herself to be petted, but she wasn't nearly as much fun as his best friend Patrick's English setter, Hot Spots. Hot Spots was a champion bird dog. If she couldn't be hunting, she loved nothing more than hanging out with Patrick and Erik, fetching a ball or a stick, or learning just about any trick they felt like teaching her.

Crenshaw was named after one of Erik's father's favorite golf champions. Mr. Carlson didn't actually play golf, but he enjoyed watching it on television, something Erik just couldn't understand. Playing golf looked slow and boring enough. Watching it on TV, with the announcers speaking in hushed voices and sounding like they were spies discussing high-level national secrets, felt to him like torture. He enjoyed *doing* stuff, like building the tree fort he and Patrick were making in the woods behind Erik's house. He preferred games where he got to *move*; to run, swing a bat, toss a ball, or shoot something.

"Mom! Dad!" he called again. "Where are you guys?"

When there was no answer he went to the living room where his parents sat, Dad in his La-Z-Boy, Mom on the couch.

"Hey, what are you doing, sitting in the dark?" Without waiting for an answer, he flipped on the light switch and continued. "Guess what! I passed! I got the highest grade in the whole class, and Patrick got the second highest. We did better than the grownups, even!"

Erik and Patrick had been taking a New York State Hunter Safety course. He waved the certificate and held up a wallet-sized card. "See? It's official! Patrick and I can go hunting with his dad! Junior hunters can go out a week before opening day, and that's this coming weekend!"

He stopped for a second to catch his breath and noticed, for the first time, the strained smiles on his parents' faces.

There was a long pause before his mother said, "It's terrific you did so well in the course, honey."

"Congratulations, Erik," said Dad. "Let me see that."

Erik handed the certificate over, and an uneasy silence filled the room. He had the feeling that although his dad was looking at the piece of paper in his hands, he wasn't really seeing it. Erik's mother's eyes were on her lap, where her hands were balled into tight fists. The air felt heavy with things that weren't being said.

"What's going on?" Erik asked.

His parents looked at each other as if trying to decide who would answer, and the silence drew out even longer.

His mother sighed, and his dad placed the certificate carefully on the table beside his chair.

"We have something to tell you, Erik," said Dad.

His mother patted the cushion next to her on the couch. "Sit down."

Erik didn't want to sit down. He didn't like the sound of this at all. A terrible list of possibilities was running through his head: either his mother or father had contracted some horrible disease, or they were getting a divorce like his friend Mark's parents, or maybe it was Erik himself who had the disease. He had just had a physical for school. Maybe the doctors had found something . . .

"I might as well come right out with it," said his dad. "We've been called up. We're being deployed to Iraq."

Erik stared dumbly at his father.

"I know how you feel, honey," said his mom. "It came as a shock to us, too. We thought that, as reservists, well, we hoped this wouldn't happen. But the war's dragged on so long"—she shrugged helplessly—"and now we're needed."

Erik was having trouble believing his ears. His parents had been staff sergeants in the Army Reserves his entire life. To Erik, it was no big deal. They each reported for duty one weekend a month. They did drills and performed fitness exercises. They took classes to update the skills the Army had trained them for. Their specialty was training other soldiers and preparing them for duty.

And, while he'd always known that there was a chance his parents would be deployed, he—and they— had never really believed it would happen. They knew other reservists who, like his parents, had been in the Army thirty years or more and never been called up. Why his parents? Why now?

As he struggled to put his chaotic thoughts into words, his father went on. "We'll be training Iraqi soldiers and MPs so they'll be ready to take over when our military leaves. It's taking longer than expected to get the locals up to speed. Lots of guys have served several tours already. So"—he spread his hands—"it's our turn, buddy."

"But—*both* of you have to go?"

"It's unusual, but, well, we've got the training, and we're needed."

There were so many questions Erik wanted to ask. "What about your jobs?" His mom was a nurse and his dad was a mechanic at a Toyota dealership.

"The hospital's already been notified," said Mom. "And your dad told the guys at the garage today. They're not happy about losing us right now, but they know it's just the way it is. We'll have jobs when we come back, honey, don't worry about that."

"But—" Erik couldn't seem to stop saying that.

"It's all very sudden, I know," Mom said, reaching over to give his hand a squeeze.

"They try to give people more notice than this," Dad said. "But we serve at the need of the Army. They can't always keep up with changing demands. An order comes down, and it's got to be met."

"How long will you be gone?" Erik asked in a small voice.

"Six months is what they're telling us," said Dad. "But that could change. It could be longer."

Erik was quiet as the enormity of his parents' news began to sink in. Finally he forced himself to ask, "What about me?"

His parents exchanged a glance. "You know the Army requires us to have a family care plan," his mother said.

Erik vaguely remembered his parents talking to him about this, but it had been a long while ago and, at the time, it hadn't seemed important. "Yeah, I guess. But I forget what it is." He had a sudden thought. "Can I stay with Patrick?"

"No, hon—" Mom began, but Erik interrupted her.

"I bet his parents would let me! I could call right now and ask."

He took a step toward the phone, but his mom said, "Erik, no. I'm sure that Patrick's mother would be happy to have you. But you know she just had the new baby, and on top of that, they've taken in Patrick's grandmother, who requires a lot of Mrs. Holt's attention. It's just too much to ask right now. Especially for such a long time."

"We have to stick to our plan," said Dad. "I'm not sure we'd even be able to change it at this point. You'll be going out to stay with Oma and Big Darrell."

Oma and Big Darrell were his mother's parents, who lived in North Dakota. Erik couldn't believe his ears.

"But I don't even know them!"

"Oh, Erik, you remember when we went out to visit," said Mom.

"I was three years old! That was nine years ago! I don't remember anything about it, and I sure don't remember them."

"Well, you've spoken to them on the phone since then."

"Yeah, on Christmas and my birthday. 'Happy birthday. How's school? Goodbye.'"

"There's no need to be sarcastic." His mother looked at him pleadingly. "Honey, the Army wants you to be with family and so do we. Your father's parents have both passed on. There's no one else."

After a few beats of silence, Erik said sulkily, "I don't even know where North Dakota is." This was a slight exaggeration. He knew it was one of those big block-shaped states out west somewhere.

Dad got out the road atlas and opened it to the map that showed the whole United States. With his finger, Erik traced the route from upstate New York, where he lived, to Fortuna, North Dakota. "That's really far," he said glumly.

"Not as far as your mother and I are going," Dad answered, in a failed attempt to sound jolly.

"How am I going to get there?"

"You'll fly out."

"How long will *that* take?"

"All day."

"All day!" Erik turned to his mother for help. "Mom, I'll go nuts sitting in an airplane all day!"

"It will actually be three different airplanes, Erik. Company resource personnel looked into it today. Your flights are booked."

Erik groaned. "What if I get on the wrong plane

by mistake and end up in . . . in . . ." He paused, trying to think of a place more remote and less appealing than North Dakota, but couldn't come up with one.

"The airline people won't let you get lost," Mom said calmly.

Erik searched his brain for another argument. Then he had it! "What about school? There's no way I can be out of school for that long. I'll get way behind in everything."

"You don't need to worry about your schoolwork," Dad answered, as if that was Erik's actual concern. "Your grandmother will be enrolling you in school out there. And your records are being sent, so they'll know which classes to put you in."

"When do I—we—have to leave?"

"You leave on Friday," Mom said quietly. "Our flight leaves Saturday morning, and we want to take you to the airport and see you off."

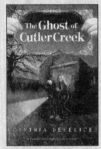